The Secrets of Cutting Grass

Blessings

T. J. Shenall

The *Secrets* of Cutting Grass

T. D. SHOWALTER

The Secrets of Cutting Grass

Copyright © 2015 by T. D. Showalter

All rights reserved. No part of this book shall be reproduced or transmitted in any form or by any means, electronic, mechanical, magnetic, photographic including photocopying, recording or by any information storage and retrieval system, without prior written permission of the author or publisher. No patent liability is assumed with respect to the use of the information contained herein. Although every precaution has been taken in the preparation of this book, the publisher and author assume no responsibility for errors or omissions. Neither is any liability assumed for damages resulting from the use of the information contained herein.

This is a work of fiction. Names, characters, places, and incidents either are the product of the author's imagination or are used fictitiously. Any resemblance to actual events, locales, or persons, living or dead, is entirely coincidental.

Cover Layout and Book Design by Wordzworth.com
Cover Photo by Diana J. Showalter

Copyright © 2015 by T. D. Showalter –TXu 1-959-200
Filed: Library of Congress, March 21, 2015, Reference # 2237221051

ISBN: 978-0-692-57717-2

Printed in the United State of America

Disclaimer

This book is fictional. This book is not intended to reflect proper practices or procedures for any of the areas of mental health, social work, the practice of medicine, law enforcement, or the practice of law; nor does the book or any of its contents represent any advice or recommendations for services, interventions, or diagnostics relative to any of these fields or any other professional activities. All characters, places, and events are fictional.

To The Reader

Intelligent, introspective, survival-savvy, fifteen-year-old Buck and his girlfriend, Harper, search for insight, courage, and meaning while their lives face life and death struggles in an unfair and difficult world. Although this novel touches on issues such as mental health, abuse, and homelessness, it is ultimately a story about Christian faith, wisdom, and finding order and meaning in the midst of chaos. Buck speaks beyond his years, but that doesn't mean his thoughts exceed the thoughts of teens. Thus, it hopes to lend a voice.

Unlike Showalter's prior book, which was generally geared to grades 5-8, this novel may be best suited for high school level readers. In addition, this book could be stimulating to those who work in the youth fields or who may be interested in a career with youth. Although aimed at slightly different reading levels, the author's two young adult novels do have common elements. One such element is the presence of an unlikely person of wisdom who lives in an unusual setting.

About The Author

T.D. Showalter spent his younger years in a small, mid-western community located in and around Savannah and Helena, Missouri. Please note that the author does not claim to have grown up in that community. His ten sisters and three brothers, his co-workers over the years, and his many friends would all attest that he has never grown up. He also does not claim any expertise in any area, especially the area of human behavior. Although he learned much from his family, friends, co-workers, and extended education, the author's understanding of human behavior continues to fall short and hold many mysteries. In spite of his lack of expertise and the risks involved, this novel and his prior novel, *Dang It, Murphy,* venture into this area.

Although the author's formal career reflects a very short, failed stint as an inner-city youth minister in the late 60's, most of his career was spent with an urban court justice system in Wyandotte County, Kansas City, Kansas beginning in early 1969. During his nearly thirty-seven years with the court, he held many positions including that of Director of the "Juvenile Court", which he held for more than two and one-half decades. His tenure with the court also reflects seven additional years as The Chief Court Services Officer. As Chief, he continued his responsibility for the juvenile court's probation and child abuse services and added the domestic relations and adult probation departments. The author retired as Chief CSO from the court system in December of 2005. Each of these positions and each person he met along the way taught him many things about life and much about himself. This is especially true of his fellow workers and the families he encountered in the court system.

Post retirement finds the author with many hobbies and activities with his family coming first. His wife, Diana, his two children, their spouses, and his five grandkids are the love of his life. In addition to family and writing, he enjoys cycling, home projects, reading, school presentations, and small group Bible study.

The author can be contacted for presentations and appearances at his e-mail address, tdshowalterauthor@gmail.com.

Also By T. D. Showalter – "Dang It, Murphy!"
A Novel For Middle School Students – Study Guide Included and Christian Study Guide Available Upon Request
Infinity Publishing Company
Available: Barnes & Noble, Amazon, & wwwbuybooksontheweb.com
Contact: *tdshowalterauthor@gmail.com*

Acknowledgment & Dedication

Special thanks go to several early-readers. Their comments and suggestions were critical. These special and insightful people asked questions, gave encouragement, and, believe it or not, found many errors. They include Mary Oehlert, Susan Giffen, Connie Renne, Kevin Day, Alexis Meredith, Lennette Bonnell, Steve Guss, Elana Becker, Adrianne Matlock, Jessica Springer, and DeAnn Warner. This group includes a Medical Doctor, Children's Pastor, PhD Psychologist, M.S.W., I.B. Teacher, PhD In Education, Juvenile Probation Officer, two Business Professionals, and a Homemaker.

Most importantly, my love and thanks go to my wife, Diana – Retired I.B. English Teacher, who was my primary editor and encourager.

The author also wants to take a moment to dedicate his efforts to all the people who work with families and youth, especially children and youth pastors, teachers, court services officers, protective service workers, and mental health providers. These professionals are underappreciated, underpaid, and often maligned. They are frontline warriors attempting, in many cases, to pick up the pieces and to restore broken children and families to wholeness. They do truly heroic work and represent some of the most valuable efforts in America. They deserve our praise, respect, and support.

Contents

To The Reader		v
About The Author		vii
Acknowledgment & Dedication		ix
Chapter 1	Mom Says I'm Mental	1
Chapter 2	Meeting of The Minds	7
Chapter 3	Food For Thought	21
Chapter 4	Harper's Heart	29
Chapter 5	Home	39
Chapter 6	The Theory of Friends	49
Chapter 7	Fingernails	61
Chapter 8	Knock Knock – Who's There	73
Chapter 9	Salvaged Musings	83
Chapter 10	Postmortem Examinations	93
Chapter 11	Walking With Weeds	101
Chapter 12	A Deadly Choice	109
Chapter 13	Keep It Simple	121
Chapter 14	Closed Casket – Opened Doors	129
Chapter 15	Sorting Baggage	141
Chapter 16	Cutting Grass	155
Chapter 17	Survive Or Live	163
Discussion Options		177

CHAPTER ONE
Mom Says I'm Mental

Mom dumped me out at the corner of 35th Street and 7th Street, and, as usual, whenever she brought me to the University Med Center, I would look up at the street signs just to confirm the oddity of two numbered streets intersecting. I chuckled and wondered why the two cities that had grown together had their number streets going in opposite directions. In the past, when Mom used to actually have a conversation with me, she would tell me that I over-thought things, only those weren't her words. She would say that my wondering and wandering thoughts were "nutty". She would say, "Look, it is what it is, can't you just accept it? It's really not that big of a deal." I had used each of these phrases with her at one point or another, and she would sometimes throw them right back at me. Although I seldom gave her credit for being right about something, she was probably right regarding the street names. For the most part, these few street labels really didn't matter that much as a large river separated the two cities, and most of the streets from the two cities didn't intersect at all. In fact, a secondary river between my house and the Med Center isolated this part of town even more. It was only in this unique, six-square-block area bordering the ever-expanding Med Center where they crisscrossed. I'd been told some of the history of the two cities, but still, to me, the signs seemed weird and simply out-of-place. Of course, I often felt weird and out-of-place in life and wondered about that, as well.

While in the process of getting my trusty red backpack mounted, I refocused on Mom, and I realized that she was impatiently waving my medical insurance card across the seat. She was trying to hand it to me along with another card that looked like a business card with a note written on it. She had always given me the insurance card, but she had never given me a note or a separate business card. Over the traffic noise and construction noise I yelled, "I know where to go," but, in her typical manner, she looked away. I stared at the scribbled note on the back of the business card.

A driver behind her honked his horn, and with that, Mom glanced in the rear-view mirror and started to pull away. As she did, she yelled her standard final message, "I'm going to find a place to park. You go ahead without me." As she accelerated, I heard empty beer bottles rattle together on the floor of the back seat, and I watched JJ's dirty, old, trash-filled car rumble down the street. I knew from past experience that she was not trying to find parking, and I knew that she would not stick around. I was on my own once again, which is how I had started to prefer it. Up to that point, I assumed that I had been picked up from school early in order to see a regular doctor as required by her social worker. Wrong!

The business card had the name G. F. Guss, LCMSW, Psychology Department, # 400 West - University Medical Center. Written in her now common, shaky and barely legible handwriting, the scribbled note on the back read, "See this guy at 2:00 and answer his questions. Don't be late or I'll tell JJ." Wow. She finally did it. She finally decided to send me to a shrink. I didn't know what LCMSW stood for, but I for sure knew what Psychology Department meant. I knew that JJ hated my guts and that, for some reason, he had been suggesting this, but I had thought that Mom wouldn't do it. I also knew that Mom had told a social worker that I was a problem child and that I had run away at times. The social worker had also mentioned counseling, but I was sure that she had said family counseling. At this point, it didn't matter who had suggested it, Mom was the one who was doing this to me.

Even though it was only March and still cold outside, my forehead felt sweaty, and I actually felt dizzy. I was mad, but I was also afraid. Tears swelled in my eyes. I wanted to run, but I didn't really know where to go. I found myself walking in the front door of the new lobby of the Med Center and looking at the clock. It was 1:30 in the afternoon on Friday, March 20th, and all I was thinking and muttering was, "My Mom thinks I'm mental."

As much as I wanted to turn around and leave, I didn't know what I would do or where I would go. If I went home without following Mom's instructions, JJ would go off, especially if he had stopped at a bar on the way home. Mom would do the same, especially if she had met JJ at the bar like she often did. Even worse than dealing with their anger, they could follow through on their threats to get me kicked out of school, the one place where I felt I belonged. I didn't know how they would get me kicked out, but they knew I cared too much about school to risk taking a chance.

Mom and JJ had first met each other at the Cisco Tavern and had made a few friends there. It had become their favorite hangout and watering hole, as she put it. Also, now that they considered my twelve-year-old sister old enough to stay by herself, they seemed to go there three or four nights a week. With all these thoughts and with all my feelings, I walked up to the information desk in a daze.

The lady at the information desk was all business. I showed her the front of the business card without saying a word, and she barked out directions like I was a new recruit in the military and she was the drill sergeant. She said, "Go to the first set of glass doors, and take the sidewalk across the courtyard to the old building. When you get inside the old hospital, follow the green line to the yellow line and then take the yellow line to the red line. When you get to the end of the red line, you will find one elevator. Take it to the fourth floor, and you will find the psych. department." She pointed with her right hand while at the same time she was saying "Next" to the person behind me. I wanted to be mad at her for seeming so abrupt and callous at a time like this, but then I realized that she didn't know what was happening to me. Of course, it could have been because there were just too many people for her to care about one fifteen year old kid.

Instead of immediately moving on like most people, I just stood in my tracks taking in all the information the clerk had just recited. Because of this, the couple behind me couldn't move forward and the clerk was leaning over trying to motion them forward. At this point, she shot me a frustrated look and shook her arm towards the glass doors and said in a bit of a louder voice, "That way, young man."

Having been dispatched, I mumbled a "thank you", readjusted my backpack, headed towards the glass doors, and quickly walked across the open courtyard and into the old building with its narrow hallways and high ceilings. I looked at the sparkling clean floor and stood still on the green line that shot off to my right side. This building was a major contrast to the bustling of the new building. The first hallway was empty, and I could only hear an echo of footsteps around the corner.

A feeling of doom was asking for attention in my gut, but instead of dealing with it, my quirky habit of wondering about details kicked in. I started to wonder why someone had chosen the color of green for directions from this particular entrance and, then, wondered, if the order of green, yellow, red, had any hidden meaning. Also, why didn't a colored line go in the opposite direction, and what would I find if I went that way? I looked up at an overhead sign and quickly realized that the opposite way would just take me to an administrative area. I decided that people who went that way probably knew where they were going. I certainly didn't. That still didn't answer all of my questions, but I started my journey down the lined hallway that was to lead me to my head shrink. I hoped he or she knew where they were going.

Again, before I even turned my first corner and, again, instead of dealing with what I was going to do when I got to the fourth floor, my mind jumped to a different matter to wonder over. As I walked, I wondered which employee they picked to paint the colored lines on the floor. Someone high up with lots of skill surely wouldn't want that job. It would seem to be beneath them. On the other hand, someone with no skills might not be the right choice either as any mistake in the lines would end up with people being lost or confused. I wondered to myself if any one else in the world would wonder about the person a hospital would choose to paint the colored lines. "Freaky! Maybe I am mental," I said out loud.

It was a quick walk to the elevator. The old elevator seemed to be waiting just for me, and I climbed aboard this narrow closet-like contraption. It took three punches of the fourth floor button before the door finally, slowly closed. Although it bumped upwards at a crawl and made some groaning noises, it seemed safe enough. Luckily, it had no terrible music playing out of a speaker. I was also thinking that I was glad I wasn't claustrophobic. I wondered if staff in this building treated claustrophobia, and if so, did those people always take the stairs. Then with aggravation, I said to myself, "Dang it, Buck, you've got enough of your own issues to deal with, so stop this." I shook my shoulders in disgust at my habit of wondering and tried to focus.

Finally, the extended zap of the old elevator buzzer sounded indicating my arrival to the fourth floor. The noise made me jump. The buzzer sounded like crossed electrical wires and reminded me of the game Operation. I hated that sound. I stepped out and found myself looking down a hallway of old, dark office doors. Over a set of double doors at the end of the hallway hung a sign with the boldly painted words, "Psychology Department – Suite 400 - W." Under the main sign, on the double doors, a number of names were listed, but I was too far down the hallway to read them. I was certain that one of the names would be G. F. Guss. I wondered what the G. and F. stood for, and hoped the "G" stood for "gullible".

My feet seemed to keep moving and before I could wonder about anything else, I was standing inside Suite 400 looking at a smiling lady who didn't seem much older than me. She actually stood up, walked around the desk, reached out her hand, and said, "Hi, I'm Margaret, but everyone here calls me Maggie. How can I help you?" I couldn't help but immediately notice that she was expecting a baby, but her movements didn't seem awkward at all. She seemed happy and welcoming and was quite a contrast to the receptionist in the lobby.

As I shook her hand, I responded with, "Hello, I'm Buck Martinez, and my Mom and I have an appointment with…" I paused and looked at the business card, "with G. F. Guss at 2:00."

The lady looked behind me and asked, "Is your Mom with you?"

I had covered for my Mom so many times in the past, that this part was well rehearsed. I went right into my routine. "She will be here in a few minutes. She was trying to find a parking spot. She doesn't get around very well. She doesn't have a handicap permit, so sometimes it's really difficult for her. I'm sure she'll be along, unless she has to make a bathroom stop. She thinks she might be coming down with the flu and felt like she might throw up."

I had a lot more lines to my practiced spiel, but that last line was enough for Maggie. She pulled her hand back, told me to have a seat, and mentioned that Dr. Guss would be back in a few minutes, as he had been called down to the E.R. for a quick consult. I was still translating that last, hurried, and jumbled sentence and wondering what exactly a consult was, when she excused herself and quickly walked to the restroom. Just as quickly, she came back. She had a paper towel and was drying her hands. She was still smiling, but she was not quite as perky. The flu comment was often an effective distraction. As Maggie returned, she picked up her remarks as though there had been no interruption. She indicated that my mom had mailed in one signed form, but other papers still needed to be completed. She handed me three additional forms, asked me to have my mom fill them out when she came in, and mentioned the need for an insurance card.

Of course, I had the medical insurance card and, with practiced timing, gave it to her for her to copy. There were only a few chairs in this entry area but no one else was waiting, so I threw my backpack onto one of the chairs, sat down in another, and started to look at the forms. I knew most of the required information and quickly filled in enough blanks to get by. They were much like the ones at my medical doctor's office and the only one that stumped me for a moment was the box asking for the patient's most recent symptoms.

This was my chance to turn the tables, so I wrote, "My 15 year old son, Buck, is a great kid and an A+ student, but he sometimes doesn't like to live with me and my boyfriend. Please don't call my house and talk to my boyfriend or tell him anything that my son says because my boyfriend is unpredictable." Actually, I thought to myself, JJ is very predictable. He's always mean, but I thought that the word unpredictable would be a good word to use to make someone hesitant to call my house. I liked picking just the right word for the right occasion. Unpredictable seemed to fit this moment for more than one reason.

CHAPTER TWO
Meeting of The Minds

After adding the note on the forms about my success as a student and the comment about unpredictable JJ, I finished the last page and gave each page one last look-over. All seemed in order, but I had second thoughts about my commentary on JJ. Finally, though, I decided that it probably didn't matter what I wrote, at least in the blanks asking for general information. I was fairly certain that no one ever really looked at most of the forms. For sure, my regular doctor's office had always skipped right to the insurance portion. In the past, I had filled out other kinds of forms, including a couple from the school that had been mailed to my house. Not once had anything ever been questioned or mentioned. Also, in this case, I didn't know what my Mom had already said, so I didn't want to bring up any new issue about me, especially about any problems. In the end, I decided to leave the comment as it was. I took advantage of that little opportunity and made sure that at least one thing good about me showed up on the record. After I handed the clipboard back to Maggie, I asked her about Dr. Guss. "So, is Dr. Guss a Psychiatrist? If not, what does the LCMSW on his card mean?"

"My, I'm not sure anyone has ever asked me that question. No, he's not a psychiatrist," Maggie replied calmly. "Gordo, I mean Dr. Guss just finished his PhD, his doctorate, in social work or psychology, I think, and his business cards are out-of-date. The LCMSW means licensed clinical masters in social work or something like that. It's just a complicated title that says it's legally OK for him to counsel with people and get paid for it. In fact, Dr. Guss still prefers us to call him by his nickname or by Mr. Guss. To be a psychiatrist, a person has to be a medical doctor, and he is not that."

"Oh, OK," I said, acting like I understood all of that.

Without looking the papers over, she placed them all into a green folder and placed the folder in a tray on top of a file cabinet right outside an office door. Immediately after that, she turned and, again, walked quickly to the restroom. I assumed that, with her pregnancy, she didn't want to catch the flu. I felt a bit guilty, thinking that maybe I should have used one of my other excuse speeches for Mom's absence, but I was a bit off my game. Next time, if there was a next time, I'd use a different cover story.

I was wondering why my folder was green when I heard loud voices in the hallway. A man was hollering at a guy named Rich about meeting after work for a tennis game. Rich answered with a laugh and, "Damn it, Gordo, you always cheat, so I don't know why I ever go with you, but, OK, I'll see you on the courts around 5:30."

The obviously good natured ribbing seemed to continue for a moment in the hallway, with the first man responding, "Just because I'm the only guy to ever beat you once or twice doesn't mean I cheat."

It certainly sounded like G. F. Guss was on his way in. My stomach turned. I looked at the door and, with the tennis comments, I imagined that the door would open and that I would encounter a tall, dark, athletic man with a short beard and wearing a conservative suit.

Instead, a man, several inches shorter than my height at five foot ten, literally bounced through the door. He had a bit of a potbelly, wire-rimmed glasses, and hair that was wild, long and a mix of blond and brown. His face was a bit reddish and flushed, but I wondered if that wasn't because maybe he had run up the steps. Regardless of that, anyone seeing the two of us side-by-side would have probably commented that we had nothing in common, at least in appearance. I was tall, had dark brown skin, and had a gangly but muscled frame topped with coal black hair.

My facial expression was flat, and I stood still. I had my eyes fixed on him with a studied gaze, and my head was cocked to one side. I intended to give him no clue about my fear, no sign of weakness. Again, his style looked just the opposite of mine. His eyes flashed around the room. His smile was wider and more exaggerated than even Maggie's smile had been. He was wearing jeans and a beach shirt with floppy sandals. He seemed to jump across the room at me, grabbed me by the right shoulder and reached for my hand to shake it. Then he laughed, looked me in the eye, and in a cackling voice, he said, "Hi, I'm Gordon Guss. You must be Buck. Where's your mom? Come on in." He didn't even wait for my answer about Mom, but maybe that was just as well.

He had bounded into his office with such energy that I was left standing and staring. At that moment, Maggie returned again from the restroom. I continued to stand and stare, as she hollered in and told Dr. Guss that my mom was parking the car. She also told him a bit of the rest of the excuse I had given. Nothing they said was quiet, but, somehow, I felt better than when I had first entered. I had assumed this would be some kind of serious atmosphere, like a courtroom or library, but instead I felt like I was in a locker room or hallway at school. Surely, someone who acted this way couldn't be all that bad, I thought. His appearance and his actions almost had me laughing. To me, he had the appearance of a short Santa Claus on vacation, instead of a head shrink.

I was still taking the whole scene in when Dr. Guss turned around and again urged me to, "come on in". Upon walking into the office, I noticed that he was looking out of a large old window. Just then, with his full arm, he motioned for me to come over and look out. As I did, I saw an enormous blue crane lifting steel beams onto a new building being constructed across the street. Dr. Guss said, "Can you believe this? I had a view that let me see all the way to the river. In a few months, all I'll be able to see is that dang wall and the street below. What do you think of that Buck, young man? By the way, why do they call you Buck?"

I waited for a moment to see if he really expected me to answer this question, and as he looked back at me, it looked like he really wanted me to respond. "Buck? Oh, because that's my real name." I thought to myself that this is a subject that I could talk about without giving away any secrets about Mom and JJ, so I added more information. "My Dad loved baseball and with the last name of Martinez, one of his favorite players was a catcher named Buck Martinez. He loved catchers and to find one with the same last name was special for him. His friends knew about this and simply started calling him Buck. My Dad also admired a couple of other baseball people called Buck, so he really liked the nickname. When I was born, he insisted that I be formally named Buck. I like it too, because, well, I like baseball, but mostly because it makes me think of my dad. I have only found one picture of him, and I think I look a lot like him."

Dr. Guss shook his head up and down as though he had taken all of this information in. He actually seemed to have enjoyed my extended answer, and then said, "Have a seat. Just sit anywhere you want."

Gee, I looked around and saw that there were five chairs in the room. I wondered if this was a test to see which chair I took and wondered if this would begin to tell him something about me. I decided to approach this whole situation like the first time I talked with some of my teachers at Summit High School. I would show him that I wasn't afraid, even though I was. So, I picked the chair right up next to his desk, put my pack on the floor in front of it and sat down with a plop. As I sat down, I took a deep breath and looked right at him. He sat down behind the desk in a large swivel chair with rollers on it and he started to look at my green folder. I guessed that this was the part where he started to decide if I was crazy or not. He looked at the folder for a good five minutes, and I could tell he really read the information. I also knew when he got to the note about JJ that I'd written, because he chuckled, looked up, and gave me two thumbs up. I blew out my breath and knew he wasn't going to be easy to con.

Then he said, "I notice that you have not once looked out the door to see if your mom has come in, even though the outside door has opened a couple of times. I'm going to guess that you don't really expect her to come at all. Am I right on this?" Definitely not an easy con!

Normally, I wasn't caught off guard. I liked to have a plan and a quick response, but his question caused me to pause so long that he chuckled. He knew that he had me. My best action or the only thing I thought to do was to shrug my shoulders and hoped he didn't press the issue. He didn't ask me about it again, but he did say, "I'm going to bet that you have covered for your mom before. You can just let me know if I'm wrong."

That just wasn't fair. It didn't give me any wiggle room to dance around the matter, and I think he knew how I felt by the look on my face. He just smiled and let out another chuckle. In my head, I said, "This guy is sharp and certainly not gullible. I kind of like him, but he's not going to be easy to outwit."

At this point, he seemed to get a bit serious and started asking me questions. His first one was right to the point with, "Why do you think your mom asked you to see me?"

Although I was thinking that I liked him, I still didn't trust him, so I kicked right back with, "Well, what did she tell you?" I decided to out-question him and get him to tell me what he knows and then just play it back to him. That was just one of the tactics in my arsenal available in dealing with adults. I was one of the best at evading, delaying, and confusing my opponent, which is how I viewed him at that moment.

His return move was another question. "Are things going well at home?"

"What do you mean by well?"

He kept plugging away with, "Well, is there a lot of stress at home, or do things seem to be going fairly smoothly?"

He just wouldn't seem to let any secret out of the bag, so I pushed back harder, "Do you always answer a question with a question?"

This time, he let out that loud cackle-like laugh and tossed the file down with, "Whoa, you've got me! You are one bright guy. Clearly, I'm not going to get anywhere with questions, unless you decide to share. Is there anything that I can do to get you to trust me even a little bit? Oh, I guess that's another question isn't it?"

I smiled a sheepish smile, took another deep breath, looked down and, then, for some out-of-character reason, I decided to tell him about the last person I had trusted with sensitive stuff. I gave him the bare minimum of information about a school nurse making a child abuse report after a teacher sent me to her office. She had asked me to "trust her" and tell her who had done that to me. Even though I had told her that I had fallen at home, she didn't seem to believe me. The next day, when I got home from school, I found out that a social worker had visited our house.

I didn't tell Dr. Guss the rest of the story, but I guessed that he already knew what I did share. It was that report that may have led to my being in his office. I wasn't about to share that JJ and Mom had been so pissed at me about the report that I took off from home and stayed with a friend for a couple of days. When I showed up a couple of days later, I told them that I hadn't accused them of anything, but they didn't believe me. I never had a black eye or busted lip again. Of course, that had not ended the problem. Again, I wasn't about to tell Dr. Guss the details. One of those details was that JJ had busted me again when I finally returned to the house. That time, however, instead of busting me in the face, he laid into my gut and ribs. Even though the social worker still came by occasionally, all she heard from Mom were stories about my misbehavior.

From then on, whenever I saw the social worker at our house, I went the other way and would never talk to her. Again, without sharing details, I ended my story with, "I learned a long time ago that there are very few grown ups that I can trust. So, if you want me to trust you with any information, you have got to promise me that you won't call a social worker about anything. If anyone ever shows up at our home again because of something I said, I'll never come back." As I said this last line, I gritted my teeth and stared at him. He seemed to know that I had meant what I said, and he nodded his head up and down with a look of understanding.

Letting it all sink in for a moment, he finally said "Whew." At that, he turned around and looked out the window for a moment, but he wasn't looking at the crane. He just seemed to stare into space. When he turned back, he said, "I can promise not to tell anything unless it involves you being abused, so would that help? We could at least talk in some general terms and get to know each other a bit. How about that being our starting point?"

"Ok, I guess we can try that," I reluctantly said.

He started off with another question, but the question had a different tone and gave me a lot of wiggle room. It was more like a request. "Would you mind just generally sharing why you think your mom wants me to see you?"

I took another deep breath and started to share. "Well, my mom is still really angry at my dad. I don't know why he left, but she says that he dumped her when I was nine years old. She doesn't even say his name anymore; she just refers to him as "that jerk" and other names that I shouldn't say. Let's see, it has now been about six years ago that he left. When she gets really mad at me, she says that I'm just like him. She seems to be mad more often now that JJ is around, and she has started calling me

"Plug" because that's what JJ calls me. He started it by saying that I wasn't worth a "Buck", and that I wasn't even worth a plug nickel. That's how he explained my not getting any gifts for Christmas. He thought the plug comment was funny. He has just kept it up ever since. At first, I didn't even know what "plug" meant, but I knew he didn't mean it in a nice way. I asked a friend what it meant and he explained that it meant a worthless, fake coin used to try and cheat vending machines. I try to ignore him when he calls me that, but it really does bug me. To me, JJ is the worthless one."

I paused just to look at Dr. Guss. It was clear that he was carefully listening and wanted me to go on. "JJ and Mom met about a year ago, but he only moved in last summer. Since Christmas, JJ has been telling my mom that I'm nuts and need to be committed. He said that if she didn't do something about me, that he would. They go out drinking several times a week and when they come home, it seems like I can't do anything right. Most nights, when I hear them drive up, I take the fire escape up to the third floor. The apartment up there is empty and I know how to sneak in. I take my school stuff, some clothes, some peanut butter, crackers, and a soda and just hang out there until they are asleep. Mom says that I run away, but I don't see it that way. Sometimes I do stay up there all night and catch the school bus the next day. " Oh crap, I thought, I've probably said too much.

"It's interesting that when your mom called last month, she didn't mention JJ." Dr. Guss was again rubbing his chin as he said this. "Go ahead, this is very helpful."

Now what do I do, I thought. It's like he wanted me to talk more. If I shared too much, I'd have dug my own grave. If I told lies, he seemed smart enough to figure them out. I started to get stressed out. Maybe if I admitted it was my problem, he would let me go. At some point I heard myself mutter and open up again like I couldn't stop myself, "Mom says I'm mental just like my dad. Sometimes she calls me other things and maybe she's right, at least some of the time. There are times I just feel so mean and mad that I think I could hurt someone. Other times, I just feel so different from others that I think I must be weird and freaky and I wonder why I'm even alive."

I went on. "When I look at things, I seem to notice details that others don't seem to see. Sometimes, I even find myself drawing some of those images, like last week when I did a drawing and painting of an old, rusty car and emphasized the detail of the rust patterns. The art teacher at Summit says that I have a gift, but, if JJ sees me draw, he says that I still like to color like a little kid. He tells me that my interests 'aren't manly.' He sometimes even yells at me to 'be like a man', which to him I think means to hit people and drink a lot. I think it's okay for a man to have interests in music and art. I used to argue with him, but I don't anymore. Now, I just try to hide my stuff from JJ."

Again, Dr. Guss turned around in his swivel chair. This time he put his elbows on his knees and his hands on his face. Then, he just sat there and again stared out the large window overlooking the street below. Finally, he looked back at me and asked me to pull my chair over to the same window. This was weird. I hoped he didn't try to hug me.

Finally, he asked, "Why do you feel different and why do you think anyone would say you are "mental," as you call it?"

Probably because I was nervous, I laughed. I had begun to think that maybe he agreed that I had a problem. In spite of that, I found myself talking more and sharing more about myself. Some of my comments were personal to the point that I had never shared them with anyone. I wasn't sure why I was so open. Other information wasn't at all sensitive and some insights were even a bit funny. Certainly those other areas of my life were not secret and were things about me that even my classmates had found obvious. "Well, for one, I ask questions about everything and find myself wondering about things that no one else seems to ask about. I also love to read, which isn't totally different, but I like to read about lots of things from sports to science. Once I even tried to read the Bible, which my mom found really strange. Anyway, I never have to be told to read." I paused for a moment, but Dr. Guss was just relaxed and listening, so I felt that it was okay to go on and said, "Another thing, I like things clean and tell my Mom how sick I am of our place being such a pit. I've told her that I would be embarrassed to ever invite a friend over. Of course, she says that I'm too weird to have friends, but that's not true. I tell her that I think JJ is a drunk and that she's too good for him, but she tells me that neither my dad nor I have any say over her life. She tells me that I'm always acting superior to her and JJ, but that I'm really just a punk. She says there is nothing wrong with having a beer or two, but I know they have a lot more than that. After she lectures me about minding my own business, she often asks me why I can't be like my sister and just accept things. In fact, when she and JJ get through with some of their yelling, I feel like I need to run away. I just don't fit into my family and sometimes wonder if I fit anywhere in life." It seemed someone had turned on my faucet of words and they were spilling over.

Finally, with my nervousness boiling over, a flurry of disconnected questions came out like vomit, one right after the other. "Do you think I'm mental? If not, why don't I fit in like others? Isn't someone paying you to fix me? What's my mom going to say when she finds out that you didn't do anything to me…like commit me to some psych place?" I ended with a gasp for air.

"Good gravy, that's quite a mouthful," he said in almost a shout. He scooted closer, looked right at me, and pointed an up-turned, open hand at me as he explained, "Yes, your mom's medical card is paying for this session, but it's up to me to determine what needs to be done and who needs to be involved. It's not up to her." He then paused, before starting again with, "Now I want to spend a moment to respond to your question about being mental and getting fixed. Those questions are good starting points if we ever hope to make any headway and if we ever want to work together on any problems. Those questions go to the heart of what I'm all about. "

Dr. Guss then stood up, crossed his arms and started walking around the room talking like he was a history teacher at Summit High School and talking about mental health as though it was the lesson for today. As he spoke, he seemed to slowly and deliberately select each word. "You need to know that I'm biased because this is an area that I love. Because of my bias, I get upset at our society for thinking about people as being strictly on one side of a line or the other. The public thinks in terms of a person being either crazy, in your words "mental," or sane and normal. Those two labels just don't hold water. Generally, a counselor is to listen as much as possible and to speak as little as possible, but I'm going to break that rule today and share some of my thoughts with you. I certainly believe that you are intelligent enough to appreciate and absorb what I'm going to tell you."

As he spoke, he put his hands together and punctuated some words by moving both hands in unison towards me as if delicately handing the words to me for inspection. "We all function with our minds so we are all mental beings. Being mental beings, at some point in life, every person will encounter at least one mental or emotional problem. There is no shame in this. Now, I'm not saying that all stress is bad. In fact, some stress in life can be good and cause us to be creative. Some problems, however, go beyond this creative stress. Some of these difficulties will represent a temporary glitch or a single traumatic life event. While others, for some people, will be considered on-going and sometimes life-long struggles."

Dr. Guss got up and went over to a small refrigerator, got himself a Dr. Pepper, and asked if I wanted one. I said, "sure" and we both took a moment to open the soda and take a drink. I could tell that he wasn't finished with his speech, so I didn't say anything else. I was glad that he was talking instead of me. I was also glad to have the drink. After another few sips, he picked up his speech as though he had never paused.

"Whether short-term or long-term, emotional events or personal life traumas are as varied as physical problems. In fact, some mental issues are partly physical. They also vary by cause as much as the physical ones.

"On the physical side of the hospital, people are seen who may only need stitches for a cut or a cast for a broken arm, while on the emotional side we might deal with a short-term depression that follows the death of a loved one. Back on the physical side, the hospital will treat a patient with leukemia or asthma that will probably impact the person for life, while, on the mental side, some people suffer from and need treatment for chronic or on-going depression and need long-term medications. The physical side also treats people for work related injuries. I see people on my side for work-related stress and even work-related trauma. Soldiers returning from battle certainly understand these issues.

"These examples can also relate to addictions. I'm sure you know that people get treated for injuries suffered in auto accidents. Some of these same people could be people that I'm seeing for substance abuse addictions.

He worked on his Dr. Pepper for a minute or two before jumping back in. "Again, my point is that the two areas are really not so different nor are they so unusual. Going back to my first point, we are both mental and physical beings. On the other hand, our society seems to be so worried about feeling mentally normal and so focused at seeing someone else as being disturbed, that we draw a line down the middle and refuse to even consider that normal is non-existent. I know that's probably more than you want to hear, so pardon me for getting on my soapbox. It's just that my buttons get pushed when I hear an individual label someone else, especially a young person. It's just not right."

Dr. Guss had stood up and wandered around some as he gave this lecture, but he sat back down and looked right at me while making his next point. It was clear that I wasn't the only one to have an open word faucet. "To answer your question and to put you at ease, I don't think you are suffering from any chronic mental illness. No, you don't need to be committed, and no, you don't need to be individually fixed. In fact, I think you are quite special, in a great way. You are so special that I'm betting that others trust you to listen to them. You know, even I have problems and even I have to decide on occasion who to trust. I get it.

"I also get that you want to fit in and be considered normal. That can be good, but it's more than okay to sometimes not fit in. Fitting in doesn't make you special, and not fitting in doesn't make you abnormal.

"Yes, there are some big-time family difficulties that you, your mom, and maybe others around you are dealing with, and I'm still thinking about what we should do, if anything. For certain, we are not going to do anything today." He looked directly at me, smiled again, and finished with, "Now, does that answer your barrage of questions?"

Except for some teachers at Summit and my friend Milo, no adult had ever said that I was special or that they thought I was trustworthy. I also picked up on several of his comments that included "we" in the mix, like the comment, "we are not going to do anything today." Those comments made me feel better and feel like I had a part in the whole process, whatever it turned out to be. I felt good and wished that I could bottle up that feeling and take it home.

I leaned in and was struggling to say something in response, but Dr. Guss, who used his hands a lot, put his hand up to stop me and said, "Before you leave today, I want to go over something one more time.

I'm concerned that I may never have the chance to share all of this in the future, so I'm going to take advantage of today. I want you to know that with all my education, I still don't have a clear idea of what normal is or if there really is such a thing. Each person is unique, thankfully, and each person has his own set of problems and issues. Some label another person's problem as weird or disturbed, but, often, in doing so, they may be trying to hide or deny their own problems out of fear or insecurity or some other feelings. You are as normal as I am, especially considering what you are going through. Now, on the other hand, you may want to know that some people think I'm weird, and they are right. I think all of us own a part of mental." He again let out his cackle. "Wow! There I go again. I think I've got a problem in that way. My kids are always telling me that I over-explain things." Even though I didn't grasp everything he said, it was clear that he meant it all and that he really cared.

In the middle of his now comforting but odd laugh, he straightened up in his chair and whirled back towards the window. As he did so, he went right on with his comments and his ever-increasing hand movements. Then, he started to zero back in on me. "I also heard you say that, at times, you want to escape or run away. Sometimes, escape can be a survival tool and it can be good. It sounds like you have had to appropriately use that tool. Yet, this thinking can also lead to thoughts of hurting yourself or a habit of not facing something you need to face. Regarding any thoughts you might have of hurting yourself, you have so much to offer in life, you are so valuable, and I want you to hear that again. So, I want you to give this whole situation some time to play out. The end results may be a long way off. Buck, you have trusted me with a wealth of information. You took a risk and I will somehow keep my word. Don't give up. Keep asking questions, keep searching, keep learning, and keep on keepin' on, and one day, you will see a light at the end of the tunnel and, no, it won't be a train coming. So, do you have any more questions or are you ready to leave?"

As I grabbed my bag, I smiled at him, "You can answer these two questions if you want. Does the "F" on your card mean that your middle name is "Francis" or "Franklin", and why do I have a green file when some of the others are brown and yellow? Are the green files just for young people?"

He chose not to answer and instead gave one last cackle and one more arm wave and loudly dismissed me by saying, "Go on. Get out of here. I'll answer those questions next week if I can get you and your mom scheduled. By the way, how are you getting home?"

I jumped out of the chair, gave him a wave, and said, "I know how to get home. Remember, I've done this part before. Before I go home though, I'm going to the cafeteria and see if I can con them out of some food. I've done that before as well." Out the door I went and didn't even look at the lines on the floor. Of course, going back to where I started always seemed easier than going somewhere I hadn't gone.

The only last wondering I did on the way downstairs was to briefly wonder what I would have said if he had asked me directly if I ever thought about killing myself. As that thought tried to jump into my head, I decided to wonder about that later.

CHAPTER THREE
Food For Thought

After I left Dr. Guss' office, I didn't wait for the slow elevator. I had appreciated its slow crawl when I entered, but after the session was over, I was ready to get out of there. With my backpack on, I bounded down the steps, back across the open courtyard, and returned to the updated part of the Medical Center. As I stood near the lobby between a set of escalators and a bank of elevators, I took a few minutes to catch my breath from my first episode ever with a shrink. I set my backpack down between my feet with one of the straps anchored around my left leg and nearest to the escalators. I tried to never let my pack out of my sight, as it had truly become my survival kit. One of the many items I kept in Big Red was a change of clothes. I was considering using one of the extra sweatshirts because I had nearly sweated through the one I had on. I wondered whether it had been my sprint back to the lobby or my nervousness with Dr. Guss. I decided not to change, as I still had to walk the two to three miles home. Besides, I thought, none of the people at the Med Center will notice, and, if they did, they probably wouldn't care.

Even though I was again enveloped by the mob of people in that general lobby area, I felt a sense of privacy that seemed counter-intuitive to the place. It was as though I was invisible to all the people around me, maybe because each of them had their own issues and simply didn't have the energy to pay any attention to me except to see me as an object to move around in a crowded area of a building.

THE SECRETS OF CUTTING GRASS

As I reflected on the exchange with Dr. Guss, I realized that it hadn't been a totally bad experience like I had expected, but it also wasn't something I would have chosen to do on my own, ever. To be honest, I actually had enjoyed part of the meeting. It ended with me having a sense of relief, but it also really took a lot of mental energy to bring up so much stuff in my life and to actually talk about it. Also, some of Dr. Guss' words were still hanging with me and I needed some time to sort through all his comments. Some of the thoughts were okay, but others felt heavy, so I tried to mentally tuck the heavy ones away. I decided that I could revisit them when I had more energy. Even then, I might just ignore some of them. All I knew for now was that the experience would be hard to describe even to my best friends, that is, if I ever even tried to share it with anyone.

As I contemplated all of this in my private mental world and ran it back and forth through my replay and wondered about each nuance of each sentence from the session, a voice from my belly rang out. At the same time, the smell from the cafeteria around the corner had penetrated my nose. My whole body had all of a sudden gone into hungry, no, famished mode. This wasn't the first time that my body found it necessary to interrupt my thinking or over thinking. I headed towards the smell.

I had some cash on me, but, for me, cash was hard to come by, and I was reluctant to spend it when other options existed. When it came to cafeterias, I definitely had other options. I just needed to decide which cafeteria strategy to execute. The end goal of each ploy was getting all the food I wanted at no cost. One common option, and the one I preferred, involved filling up a food tray, with a medium portion of exactly what I wanted, and then looking around the room for just the right couple. I would look for an elderly couple that seemed to act sweetly towards each other and, once I had spotted them, I would time my entry into the check out line so that I would be positioned right in front of that sweet-acting couple. I would smile at them, and ask them in a friendly voice, "How are you today?" Timing, selecting the right couple, friendliness, and acting out my predicament were always the key elements of this strategy.

Once I was in front of the couple and immediately after greeting them, I would begin to search my pockets and backpack for money. As I would get closer to the check out clerk, my search would become more frantic and upon reaching the cashier, I would announce, "It seems as though I've forgotten my wallet. It looks like I'll need to put this back." I had used some other lines, but the end result was to delay the couple behind me and to give them the sense that I was in a tight spot and needed someone to bail me out. If I had picked the couple correctly, this worked perfectly, and the couple would say one of two things. Each of the two responses ended with the couple, usually the lady, telling the cashier to add my total to their total. They would inevitably smile and tell me to have a great day. I would often end this interaction with a warm feeling and a thought that I had just helped someone do a good deed for the day. To reinforce the feeling, I would try to sit near the couple and visit a bit. I had always seen it as a win-win outcome and had never felt any guilt about my actions.

Unfortunately, there were very few people in the cafeteria at that moment, so I decided that I had to select a different strategy. My second option was less complicated and had no feel good part except to satisfy my hunger. Also, this second method had a higher risk of getting into trouble. I tried to think of it as my slight-of-hand method, but it was really just stealing. My first move took me straight to the seating area of the cafeteria, and, out of sight from the cashier, I located the largest, used paper cup that I could find. It wasn't difficult to be out of the sightline of the cashier as the seating area had numerous posts and several nooks and crannies. If a large cup wasn't on a table, I had no problem grabbing one out of the trash. My plan was to walk the wrong way through the checkout line, and tell the cashier that I had to get a clean cup as this one leaked. When back in the food area, I would load up two plates with one large item like lasagna, go around a corner by the soda machine, get a large clean cup and dump the lasagna into the clean cup. I would leave the tray and plate on a counter and walk back through the check out line with a clean spoon or fork and tell the cashier thanks for letting me get a new cup. For a drink, I would simply drink out of the water fountain. Sometimes, I could get three items into a single large cup. It was amazing what they could hold. This meal was not as well balanced as the meal with option one, but it filled me up just the same.

With option two selected, I had moved from the serving side of the cafeteria, returned to the hallway, and re-entered the cafeteria from the seating side. I immediately identified a tray with a large cup in the far corner and went for it, but as I neared the cup, something or, actually, someone caught my eye and I forgot all about being hungry.

Even though her back was to me and her head was tilted, I easily picked out the profile of Harper as she leaned her head on one bare arm. With her thin build, light black to dark brown silky-smooth skin, and jet-black, tightly curled, almost kinky hair, she seemed to be a one-of-a-kind beauty, at least to me. Besides her stunning looks, I considered her to be my best female friend and the one I talked to the most. Our friends considered us a couple, and I sometimes said that we were "going together", but with no car, no cell phone, and little money, there was a limit to how far we could go. Harper could hold her own on most any topic when she spoke, but she also was a great listener. My only conversational frustration with her was that it was difficult to get her to share about herself, especially her feelings. She seemed to prefer to listen rather than talk.

Upon seeing her, I loudly announced my presence across the seating area, "Hey, Harpo. What in the world are you doing here?" All the kids at school called her by her middle name, Elise or Ellie, which she told them she preferred. Yet, after I found out that her first name was Harper, I couldn't resist using it. So, I had started calling her either Harper or Harpo, especially when others weren't around. She had, at first, acted put out when I used Harper or Harpo, but it had become clear by her smiling responses that she at least didn't mind. I seemed to be the only one who could get away with using it.

Harper had been swirling her cup around in slow motion, but when she heard me, she slammed the cup down, and, with a surprised look, quickly swirled herself around to face me. She simultaneously flashed that delightful smile. I had once told her that her smile could surely power a solar panel on its own, if ever needed. In a weaker than usual voice, she called back with, "Hey Bucko. What in the world are you doing here?" Her question had emphasized the word "you".

"I asked you first," I said as I excitedly jogged over to her table. When I got to the table, I wanted to hug her, but, earlier this school year, in an odd move, she had stopped allowing me to hug her. She had given very specific instructions to me about how we should greet physically. I think my hugs had become a bit too personal. So, as usual, she followed her established protocol. She grabbed my left wrist as I grabbed her right one. Then, she affectionately stroked my right arm and shoulder with her left hand. When she first put a stop to any full embrace, I was offended and had asked her what was up. She had sheepishly explained that it was her problem, and that each time she saw me, she was tempted to do more than just hug. She said that she had to keep me at arms length to protect us both. So the arm grab had become our signal to keep our physical contacts at arms length. I knew exactly what she was talking about, but I had mixed feelings about this restriction. I respected her and her beliefs even more, but I also felt that it represented a lack of trust. In the end, her sweet stubbornness won out.

That day, her arm's-length greeting seemed different than usual as her grip seemed to last longer, and her arm rub became more of a grab. As the greeting ended, she sat down, and, once again, picked up her cup and started nervously swirling it. Only then did I notice the wet tissue, some redness in her eyes, and puffiness in her cheeks. I felt like a dummy realizing that most people come to the hospital when either they or someone they care about are sick. My stomach turned as I thought about what had made my Happy Harper cry. "Hey girl, what's going on? Are your mom and dad okay? Where are they and why are you down here?"

She stopped swirling and looked me in the eye, "Mom and Dad are upstairs in a consult with a doctor and getting some more information about a test that was just completed. They sent me down here to get something to eat, but I just didn't feel hungry. They gave me this twenty-dollar bill to buy some dinner. Would you like to sit down and have dinner with me? It would mean a lot to me if you would hang out with me for a bit." I found it interesting and a bit unnerving that it was the second time within hours that I had heard the word consult.

It was also unnerving that my focus could change in such a short time. Only minutes earlier, I had been trying to manipulate a way to get a free meal and would have jumped at any offer. Instead, I hesitated. I wanted more information immediately, but could see that she wasn't ready to share much, so I replied, "I'd love to stay and I will absolutely eat with you, but only if you'll eat something too." It seemed that I was always telling her that she needed to eat more. In the prior weeks, she was always tired and just hadn't looked right.

THE SECRETS OF CUTTING GRASS

She agreed, and, without speaking, we went together to the serving side of the cafeteria. We each picked out a light meal and a drink, used Harper's twenty to pay, and returned to the table. I had no guilt over Harper paying for the meals, as I knew her dad and mom would welcome me, and I knew that the twenty did not stress their budget, especially with the jobs her parents each held. Harper's father, Mr. Hawkins, had, at one time, been a hospital administrator, but now he owned and operated a funeral home. Mrs. Hawkins also worked. Although she had once been a full time nurse, she had only done nursing part time since Harper's adoption.

When we returned, Harper sat across from me and started to nibble on her food. She also seemed to be breathing hard, but I thought that she was just nervous about something. I decided to eat and give her some time to share. Up to this point, I assumed that the doctor and the test involved her dad or her mom, but as she started to share, it was clear that she was the one who had just undergone the test and that she was the one in trouble. Her dad and mom were upstairs getting additional details regarding the next step. She had not yet shared what the illness was, but she wouldn't be this upset unless it was serious. Harper paused, looked at me again, sighed, and then said, "So, it's your turn. What's going on with you?"

I nearly choked on the question and my food. For a moment, I had forgotten my mental gymnastics of the day, and had no idea how to share any of it with the one girl who I wanted to think the best of me.

Since I was asking her to trust me, I decided to trust her. She already knew a lot about my mom and JJ and some of the problems, and she knew about my frequent escapes to the third floor of my apartment building. She was also aware of some of their threats to take me out of school at Summit if I ever accused them of anything. On the other hand, I had not talked about the threats to take me to see a shrink nor had I shared about them saying that I was mental and how they had continued to accuse me of being "nuts". This was going to be uncharted trust territory, but I decided to plunge ahead. I figured if I didn't share, she wouldn't tell me what was really going on with her.

I finally blurted out, "My mom thinks I'm mental, and sent me to see a shrink today. She was supposed to come too, but, as usual, she skipped out and left me holding the bag. I just came here from that office. Dr. Guss, the shrink, said that he didn't think I was mental, at least in that way, and, in fact, said that I'm pretty special. I actually liked the guy, and I think he liked me."

Harper reached across and grabbed my hand and said with intense anger, "You've got to be kidding! That's the most ridiculous thing I've ever heard. She and JJ are the ones who are nuts. Someone needs to just grab them, shake them, and tell them to get a clue. I just can't believe it. Well, maybe again, considering who it is, I guess I can believe it."

She paused for just a moment and then changed her tone. "You know this past year, there have been times when I thought I was going crazy, but I didn't want to tell you or anyone else. I also didn't tell you about all the tests and how I've been feeling. I'm so tired of being sick and sick of being tired, but most of all, I'm really sick of being prodded and poked. Some days, I just want to scream. There's no way you're mental. That doctor is right, you are special in many ways, especially the way you put up with your mom and JJ, and he probably doesn't even know the half of it. Oh, Buck, I'm so sorry that you are going through this. Someday, it's going to be different, I promise. How are you doing with this?"

I was caught off guard by the intensity of her attack mode and her sympathy, so I joked, "Ok officer, I know she hit them with a bat, but she didn't mean to kill them." Then more seriously, I said, "Wow, I think you would really go to bat for me. And, I think you even like me a bit." Of course, her speech on my behalf and the fact that she had listened so well made me like her even more. Finally, I responded to her question and said, "I think I'm doing okay. Nothing really has changed." Then, I felt a rush of anger that surged into words. "This is just part of the same old insane chaos and crap I live with. I really don't know how much longer I can put up with this shit. I just can't seem to come up with any option. I feel like I'm stuck in a sewer."

Even though she completely understood the specific source of my anger, she didn't like me using words like that. On that occasion, except for a slight frown, she overlooked the short-lived slip-up. There had been times in the past where my anger and feelings about Mom and JJ had burst into an extended verbal tirade, but, that day, I controlled it fairly well. I was fortunate to have Harper to vent to. She was one of the few people I trusted with some of my deepest feelings. Some of these feelings seemed to simmer in a realm just beneath the surface, and sometimes, they seemed to take on a life of their own. With certain unknown triggers, they could jump out and take on the appearance of either rage or depression. Although I could push them back down, I couldn't seem to ever destroy them. I was glad the most sensitive ones hadn't slipped out earlier that day with Dr. Guss.

There was a pause in the conversation, as we both seemed to collect our thoughts and catch our breath. It provided a natural stopping point, and I didn't really want to go any further on that subject anyway. Thinking about Mom and JJ just took me in mental circles and usually made me even angrier, so I thought it best to avoid any extra thinking about them and my feelings. Besides, I felt that I had shared enough to, at least, allow me to get back to questioning her about why she was in the hospital and to ask what these tests were all about. At the time, I didn't realize that her issues would take my mind completely off my problems.

CHAPTER FOUR
Harper's Heart

I leaned towards her, took her hand and gently said, "Harper, I've shared, now quit avoiding me. I know when someone's beating around the bush. I'm the best at bush beating and that's exactly what you've been doing. Now, tell me. What's wrong? Please, don't leave me hanging. Please, tell me what's going on and tell it all."

Harper, still acting a bit out of breath, took a quick breath or two and, with tears in her eyes, started to give details about her health. She reminded me of her adoption when she had been two years old, and that it was a private adoption. At the time, Mr. and Mrs. Hawkins weren't aware that she had a genetic heart problem. They found out shortly after when they took her for her first check-up. Everyone knew they would have adopted her either way, but the news of this serious health issue really shook them up. They had told Harper many times that they were scared to death back then. They felt so thrilled to get her and considered her to be the best thing that ever happened to them. They just couldn't stand the thought of turning around and losing her. As Harper told this part, she beamed.

It took several months after the initial discovery to determine the extent of the heart defect and to figure out the best course of action. Harper wasn't able to explain all of the medical details, but went on to say that a decision was finally made when she was nearly three years old to delay open-heart surgery, as the risks seemed too great. The doctor back then felt that the problem could possibly correct itself as she aged or that perhaps it, at least, wouldn't get worse. She hadn't been in any immediate danger. Also, the doctor had looked at all the new treatment options that were becoming available and told her mom and dad that maybe some new avenues would open up to even make a procedure easier. That decision seemed to be a good one as all was well until early last fall.

Unfortunately, things changed and her health had become an issue. No one, however, immediately suspected that it was her heart. Shortly after the beginning of school, she started feeling slightly worse and that led her to drop off of the swim team. She described feeling weak and extremely tired and couldn't seem to catch her breath after swimming even one lap. Mr. and Mrs. Hawkins thought that maybe she was coming down with the flu or some other virus. They also considered that maybe it was hormones because she had described, in her words, feeling puffy. At the time, she even joked about her swimsuit not fitting like she liked it to. When the problems persisted for the next few weeks, and when no one else seemed to come down with the flu, they took her to her pediatrician. The pediatrician immediately referred her back to her pediatric cardiologist who had not seen her for some time. Appointments with specialty doctors were difficult to schedule and she didn't see the first heart doctor until a month ago. Harper's regular heart doctor was a lady named Danielle Mills, whom Harper loved. Dr. Mills indicated that Harper's heart wasn't working right, and that one side of her heart seemed slightly enlarged. The hole in the heart that was originally diagnosed had not seemed to be larger, but neither had it become smaller. More importantly, that hole was now causing serious problems. It would need to be fixed and the sooner the better. Harper's symptoms were caused because her blood simply wasn't being pumped efficiently nor was the blood receiving the oxygen needed. The heart was now reacting negatively. Dr. Mills referred her to a heart surgeon for additional tests.

Clearly, all of the tests that were necessary for the final diagnosis and probable surgery had been difficult for Harper to endure. She called them torture. She hated needles, hated the feeling of being confined in some of the machines that did the scans, and generally just hated getting poked and prodded. She explained that, some not only hurt, they made her feel that life was out of control and that she was completely vulnerable.

Although I hurt for her as she detailed some of the tests, in the end, I wasn't as concerned about them as I was concerned with what she next told me.

Yesterday, Harper's shortness of breath had become more severe. Dr. Mills agreed to see Harper immediately and found that the heart was under way too much stress. She also found a significant fluid build-up in the body. It was the fluid that was causing Harper to feel puffy and also part of her shortness of breath. She was concerned that this could eventually lead to heart failure. Dr. Mills had called the surgeon from her office and a consult had been set for today to confirm the need for open-heart surgery and to probably schedule it. Although Mr. and Mrs. Hawkins wanted to make sure there were no other options, the only real question was how soon the surgery would be scheduled. When the doctors told Harper this, she asked to leave the room and let her parents finish the meeting. There was also some paper work to be taken care of. So, Harper was in the cafeteria trying to process all of this and trying to cope with her fears and her feelings of vulnerability.

"Wow! Unbelievable! How could you sit there and let me tell you all about my troubles when all the while you had this kind of news? I couldn't have done that. Harper, I've never known anyone that unselfish."

"I agree. I'm great…not. At least I have my family's support. You just keep getting dumped on."

"Yeah, but I've got you, and that's even better." Although she released a weak smile when she heard this, her hands fidgeted. I knew she was afraid, but I asked the question anyway hoping that she would share.

"I think I'd be scared. Are you afraid?"

"You better believe it. I just can't imagine any part of it without cringing. I can just see my body lying naked on a cold table while some old guy cuts my chest open. Then, he puts his hands on my heart. It hurts just to think about it." As she shared this, her shoulders seemed to shudder. "Even worse, if I do wake up, I'll have a tube in my throat. I know it's to help me breathe, but I just think I'll choke on it. I think I'll panic before the operation and run out of the operating room."

"Dang, I never thought about all of that. I think I'm going to be sick. I told one of my science teachers that I thought I might want to be a doctor someday because it sounded interesting to work on bodies, but seeing it as working on people like you and not just bodies makes me wonder if I could ever do that. Have you ever thought about asking the doctor to warm the table and his hands before the operation?"

"Dang it all, Buck. Now, I'm going to be sick. Oh, I guess I already am. You know good-and-well that the cold is the least of my worries. Buck, I'm afraid of dying. I would miss everyone most, but I also think it's just so unfair. I think it sucks, but I don't say that to my folks. I want the chance to be something special. I sometimes dream about becoming a great artist or musician or teacher, but now I worry about not getting a chance to have any dream come true."

"My dreams are usually nightmares, unless I dream about food. Speaking of food, aren't you hungry? Now, don't get mad, you know I'm teasing."

"Buck, sometimes you're just another guy. I do believe that if you ever became a doctor, you could eat in the middle of an operation. That's one gross thought, but at least, you're taking my mind off me."

"What was that noise?"

"It's another text from Corina. She wants to know what's up, but I don't know what to tell her or how to tell her. I need someone to pray for me, because I can't seem to do anything except feel panic, but I can't ask her to do that without telling her the whole story. I'm just not ready to do that right now."

"Well, I'm glad you'll ask her to do the praying and not me. You know how I feel about that God stuff." I had told her when we started seeing each other that I wasn't a "churchy". I explained that I wasn't going to pretend to pray when I didn't even know if God existed. I had asked her, if God really exists, why does he let such bad things happen to people? I wanted the best for our relationship, but I wasn't going to fake it.

"I know, I know how you feel, but right now I just can't deal with all of this on my own, and God is real to me. Besides, I wasn't asking you anyway. I hope that someday you'll look beyond your so-called survival skills and admit that you don't know it all." She looked a bit angry as she said this, and I realized that I had talked when I should have been listening.

As Harper stopped talking, she crossed her arms over her chest, and looked around the room as if looking for help. Finally, she rushed to my side of the table, disregarded her arm's-length policy, fell into my arms, and with tears, she rolled out more feelings. "I just can't even think about how my parents will deal with all this, especially if I die. They would be devastated. I don't want to do that to them. I'm not afraid of where I'll go when I die, I just can't fathom being without my family and my friends. The thought of death seems so lonely that I shake as I even think about it. Buck, I don't know what to do. I want to live!"

I was suddenly unable to speak and, each time I had even an impulse to speak, I flushed the words down my mental drain. Each sentence attempt was immediately measured as another wrong and stupid comment. It came to me that I finally and completely understood the word "dumbfounded", as I felt like an idiot and found nothing to say. I hugged her back and realized that I was crying too. Finally, I heard a voice say, "Dang it, I want you to live, too, and you will." It took me a moment to realize that it was my voice. With that said, I sat silently with her for the next five minutes, and, for one of the few times in my life, I had nothing else to say.

In any other circumstance, I would have enjoyed breaking her rule and would have relished the opportunity to hug her, but this situation was just all kinds of awkward and uncomfortable. I liked to think I was smart, but life kept throwing things at me that I couldn't fix. I thought, "Damn my life. This is the final straw." I had thought it couldn't get any worse, but it just had. I was hurting, but I was also mad. I wanted to hit something.

Harper sat up, looked at me, and cupped my face in her hands. She said, "You are so special to listen to me like this. I think God had you come at just the right time to be here with me. My special Bucko." I was still speechless and wondered how God got back into this. I just shook my head and was in the midst of feeling an even dumber dumbfounded when both she and I heard someone walking up to us. It was her mom and dad.

My initial reaction was to almost dump Harper out of my arms and to stand up at attention. I hadn't known what to expect, but it certainly wasn't for them to welcome me into sharing in the family bawl session, but that's exactly what happened. They walked right up to Harper and me and both embraced us in a group hug. Stepping back, Mrs. Hawkins grabbed my arm and said, "Buck, it's so nice of you to be here with Elise at a time like this. Your timing is perfect. Elise has always told us that you are special, and now we know that's true. Thank you."

For just a split second when her mom said "Elise", I was surprised enough to turn my head to the side and open my mouth. I had forgotten that Harper had told her parents as well as the school that she wanted to be called Elise or Ellie. I quickly adjusted and was able to stumble out some words, "You are welcome, but I didn't know anything about this, I was just here to ah…" but the words again wouldn't come. Just an hour before, I had been a verbal wizard with Dr. Guss, but at that point I couldn't even put a sentence together.

Harper jumped in with perfect timing to keep me from revealing why I had been at the hospital. She said, "Buck was going to get something to eat when we saw each other, so we had dinner together. Even better, Bucko has taken the time to listen to me whine and feel sorry for myself. You're right, Mom, he is special." She was wiping her eyes and trying to smile and give her parents a show of strength. It wasn't a perfect acting job, but it got us through the awkward moment.

Harper's dad picked up the conversation saying, "Thank you, Buck. This has been a tough day for us. In fact, it's been a tough few weeks and we've got another tough bit to go, but we will get through this together. We are a strong family." Although he said this with conviction, each word had come out slowly as though he was struggling and juggling too many issues in his head at once.

I finally was able to complete a couple of sentences without stumbling and said, "Mr. and Mrs. Hawkins, I'm glad I was here. I'm afraid I've not been of any help. All I could do was listen. I knew Harper was not feeling well, but I had no idea it was her heart. I'm sorry that I hadn't realized that all of this was going on. I feel like a jerk. I would be glad to get out of your way if you all need to talk."

Mrs. Hawkins patted me on the shoulder as she sat down and said, "Please call us Max and Lucie. We consider you a good friend of Ellie's and would welcome you to sit with us for a moment. We need to tell Elise what was decided and prepare ourselves for the next step."

With that, we all moved to a round table and Mrs. Hawkins continued. "Elise, we have accepted the doctors' recommendation to get this surgery done as soon as possible. Both doctors have said it is urgent. They have a special operating suite for cardiac surgery and they have an opening on Monday. We have told them to schedule you. Even though tomorrow is

Saturday, we are to call them in the morning to confirm some things and receive preparation instructions. Waiting any longer puts you at serious risk for heart failure and that's just not acceptable. Yes, there are risks with the surgery and it's not going to be a fun week, but this surgeon does these kinds of operations all the time and has a great success rate. We just have to trust their expertise, but, just as much, we need your support and agreement. You heard most of what they had to say, and we think you agree that this is really our best hope and option, but we are not going to drag you back in handcuffs and make you do this. Not only do we want your approval on this, we need you to have a determined optimism about this. Your commitment to this and your attitude can make a big difference in overcoming this obstacle. We have preached that approach all our lives and we are not going to change now. What do you say?"

I looked at Harper who seemed to have her head bowed and hands clasped as though she was praying. When I looked back at her mom and dad, they had begun to mirror Harper's posture. Again, I sat there like a dummy. I certainly wasn't going to bow my head, but I had no idea what to do. Although their silence ended within seconds, it seemed like five minutes. It ended with Harper letting out a big sigh and saying, "I know you are right and I am committed. I agree it's the only thing that makes sense. I'm just scared. When you call them tomorrow, will you ask them to make sure that Buck and Corina can visit me as soon as possible?" Although Harper had several really great girl friends, Corina Schuler was her best, best friend.

"You bet, Critter," said her dad. I had never heard him call her that, but it was clear from Harper's smile that this was a special name of affection. "Buck, do you want me to call you tomorrow and let you know what's up?"

"Well, Sir, I don't have a phone, but I'll get ahold of you or Corina. If that's okay with you?" It was obvious that Harper had never shared much if anything about my crazy home life with her dad, and now certainly wasn't the time. My mom had a cheap Trac phone, but she never let me use it, and I couldn't afford one of my own. I was left with always bumming from others.

Harper's dad nodded with understanding and said, "Fine. We will get the show on the road. What do you say, Critter, would you like to get on home and get some rest?"

"Sure, Daddy. Could we give Buck a ride? We go right through Armourvale on the way to our house and you can just drop him at the McDonald's there. It's only a couple of blocks from his house." McDonald's was actually about eight blocks from my house and Harper knew that, but I realized that she was only trying to think of an easy place for him to let me out and was trying to save me the possible embarrassment of being let out in front of my unpredictable, insane home.

Again, her Dad said, "You bet." Our group trudged quietly to the parking lot, loaded into the large, black SUV that looked like one of Mr. Hawkins' newer funeral home vehicles. Once buckled in, we quickly exited the multi-story parking garage.

As we drove past the Med Center, I found myself looking out the window and noticed that I was again at the corner of 7th and 35th. Mr. Hawkins was preparing to turn north on 7th street and ready to head towards Armourvale. Although it had only been hours since I was dumped out at this intersection, it seemed like ages ago. At that moment and at that intersection, it seemed that both time and numbers were warped. Never in my life had I experienced so much in such little time. It seemed like a dream or maybe a nightmare.

As we headed north across the Prairie River Bridge, it seemed that Harper had regained her composure. We held hands across the back seat and sat in silence. As I prepared to exit the SUV, she grabbed my wrist as usual, but, of course, nothing seemed usual any more. The door opened and the cold evening air hit my face as I glanced up at the lights surrounding McDonald's. We waved and said our goodbyes and the Hawkins family was off and on their way to the somewhat exclusive, old, neighborhood of Indian Heights.

As I watched them drive up the hill and over the rail yard viaduct, I felt a feeling of loneliness and darkness that surpassed any of the previous periods of darkness in my life, and I had experienced many. I turned towards the place called home, the place that had nothing in common with the word "home" in the dictionary. As I kicked an empty beer can down the dirty, broken sidewalk, I wondered why I was going to a place where I certainly wasn't wanted. I had to admit that I had no place else to go and kept on walking. Each step was a burden. I felt so tired, but it wasn't late.

It was obvious to me that Harper wanted to live and that she had everything to live for. For me, though, I couldn't imagine how I could live the next couple of years like this, especially in the same house with Mom and JJ. If Harper didn't make it, I would make sure that I wouldn't either. If she did, well, I guess I'd think about that later. Harper had said it best, "It's just not fair." That's how I felt. On one hand, Harper had a physically damaged heart. On the other hand, she had a perfect heart for people and she certainly deserved to live.

As I turned west onto Sage Drive, I saw Milo ahead setting next to a rough-looking, wooden fence with brush wrapped around the blackened post. Milo's feet were resting on an empty, wooden box. I decided to at least say hello to my homeless friend before finishing my walk home.

CHAPTER FIVE
Home

As I neared Milo's sentry position at the entrance of the homeless camp along the Prairie River, I realized that he was asleep and snoring as he sat in the over-sized, executive chair that had been retrieved from someone's trash. As usual, during the cold months, Milo was wearing his red stocking cap and a long black coat. Also, he was wrapped in a large old blanket. An inexperienced observer of this unmoving object would probably not guess that a human being rested under this pile. As the footrest on the chair didn't work, Milo had his feet covered with his surplus Army boots resting on an old crate. Milo kept watch at this key entry point until late in the evening and would generally restrict entry to the regulars. Occasionally, he would allow a transient to set up camp for a short time or allow a new longer-term entry, but he was a sharp judge of character and had his standards. I knew that later each evening, Milo would retreat to the inside portion of the camp, check on several of the tenants, and eventually settle into his own tented creation that he called home.

The camp was in a somewhat isolated area nestled among some large trees and a few scrub trees along the north side of the river but on the south side of the levee. It was visible from the river, but otherwise, it was out of sight. The smaller trees were helpful for tying up tents and for providing a windbreak. They also provided a bit of privacy from tent to tent and from the outhouse. The outhouse wasn't really a structure as much as it was a designated area. It consisted of a stack of broken, wooden pallets covering a hole in the ground. The whole contraption was surrounded on three sides by a tarp and the open side faced the river. One of the tarps covered the top, at least partially. As for the shelters, most were flimsy tents and cardboard lean-tos. Milo's was the exception.

There was seldom any traffic or movement along this poorly maintained stretch of Sage Drive. One exception was the routine police patrol. Also, two individuals from a church would drop by on a regular basis with bundles of helpful necessities. They visited, but Milo said they didn't preach. He appreciated them and said that their consistent actions spoke louder than words. For the most part, though, outside contacts were rare and, generally, not welcomed. This was especially true during some of the holidays. Milo called them the "one and done holiday do-gooders". He described them as coming to peel off some guilt by passing out a few items and, all the while, passing out too much advice. Milo, in particular, would say that he had enough guilt on his own, and he didn't need more. Besides, he would say, "My bad habit isn't going to be corrected by advice from them."

Homeless camps probably weren't legal, but the police were well aware of Milo's camp, and they acted like they were okay with it. This seemed especially true as long as Milo was in charge. Each evening, if the normal patrol nightshift had time, a car would swing by and give Milo a wave. Occasionally, they would hand him a cup of coffee and a doughnut and shoot the breeze for a few minutes. Milo seemed to appreciate the cops and, in turn, they seemed to enjoy him. At times, it looked like a mutual admiration society.

Some of the veteran police officers referred to Milo as "Mayor Milo". They had first known Milo from their contacts with him when he had often appeared as a defense attorney on cases they'd been involved in. It had been nearly a year since he had last appeared, but they remembered him as Michael Logan, one of the brightest and most honest attorneys in town. In fact, the cops wouldn't hesitate to ask Milo for informal advice about a personal legal question or advice about which attorney to call. They never forgot that he had a serious drinking problem that had interrupted his successful law practice, but, regardless, they respected him for what they deemed his uncanny insight and honesty. They also admired the fact that he had quit taking clients on his own. Although he had never come to court under the influence, Milo admitted that he had started coming without his normal preparation. He couldn't stand himself for that. Again, like entry into the camp, Milo had his standards, and he applied them to himself.

As I walked closer to Milo's, I wondered why I felt such friendship with him while, at the same time, felt such venom for JJ and even sometimes towards my mom. Each of them had drinking problems, but they were totally different people. I wondered what made the difference.

"Hey Milo, it's Buck coming up on you. Did I wake you?" I knew that I was going to wake him up, but this gave him a bit of warning about my approach so that he wouldn't be startled and mistake me for a threat.

Milo coughed, sat up, and stretched his arms and responded wearily, "Hey back, Buck. Isn't it pretty late to be getting home from school?"

"No Sir, I just had doctor's appointment. Just thought I'd swing by and say, "hi". Is all well at the camp tonight?" Milo had told me that I never needed to call him "Sir", but I often did it anyway, out of respect.

"Yup, doing fine. It's not quite as cold as it's been, so I've been sleeping better these days. As much as I don't like the cold, it's better than the bugs, so I'll take it. You still having a tough time with that low-life your mom's been hanging with?"

I wasn't ready to talk about it. "Oh, let's not talk about that tonight. Today's been a full day, and I'd better get on to my house. I need to stake out my area before they get home, if they're not home already. Mind if I drop by tomorrow? Maybe, I'll give you an update then. I could sure use your advice on a couple of things."

He grunted, "You know you're welcome here anytime, but I sure hope I'm not your only source of advice. Some people think I'm a poor excuse for a person, so beware."

I laughed and said, "Yeah, I know you come with your own warning label, but you seem to see things that I overlook, so I'll stick with you."

He nodded and said, "Okay, Buck. See you later," and curled back up like a rubber band resuming its original shape.

I walked on down the street while I kept an attentive eye open for any movement. Although I felt fairly safe, I realized that trouble could spring up at any time. The ability to stay tuned-in no matter the circumstance was a great survival skill in any city. I knew that as long as I didn't get in the middle of two gangs competing over turf, a drug buy, or a burglary, I was okay. There had been a couple of break-ins at some businesses in this area, including one last year at Manny's, a gas station and convenience store. Manny's was the place where I picked up a few hours of work each week. Overall, I had a good nose for anything out of the ordinary. I also had my own practiced way of blending in and being almost invisible in my part of town. I wished that I could be invisible at my house at times, but I knew I'd never blend in. From JJ's perspective, I was a freak of nature.

As I walked by the closed door of a dilapidated garage, I heard some people inside. It sounded and smelled like "druggers". Most of us in this neighborhood, even the gang bangers, called these people "zombies" or the "walking dead". Their glassy eyes, skinny bodies, rotten teeth, and pockmarked faces gave them away. That evening it smelled like they were smoking dope. I could also hear the rubber snap against their arms in preparation for shooting up. Their drug of choice was probably Meth. It used to be other drugs, but Meth seemed to be the newest and most deadly. Their addiction seemed to me like a torturous method of committing suicide. If I ever checked myself out, and I had thought about it, I certainly wouldn't want to take my mind first. When I saw them, all I saw were desperate idiots. I had certainly felt desperate many times, but I told myself, I never wanted to be seen as an idiot. I hurried my steps and moved by quickly. The "druggers" were as unpredictable as JJ.

My part of town has always been referred to as Armourvale. It may have been its own town years ago, but I wasn't sure. Whether a formal town or not, it had been gobbled up by Freeman City. Ultimately, a number of other small towns and neighborhoods were merged, making Freeman City the second largest city in the area. Most people were still aware of Armourvale's uniqueness and history. People were also aware of some unique history about the other, by-gone sections of town. In each case, those towns, with names from the past, were much like the people in them. Their legacies included infamous baggage along with rich histories.

Armourvale was named after one of the larger of the beef packing plants that had been located in this small valley between the rivers and the railroads. When the plants were active, the line workers, mostly immigrants from Europe, lived in the valley near the plants, while management and white-collar workers lived up on the river bluffs that surrounded the valley. Although the beef plants had long been closed, the stigma and class division associated with the second tier status of this area seemed to continue. In recent years, immigrants continued to move in and out of my area, but most of them were from Mexico, which is where my dad was born. The area felt land-locked as the rail yards were on the north side and the other three sides were cut off from other parts of town as the Prairie River made a semi-circle that started on the west side, swept in an arch around the south side and then connected to a larger river on the east side. Sometimes, I felt locked in, too.

My plan and opportunity to escape from Armourvale had roots in my success at Riverside Elementary School. Several incredible teachers at that school had shown interest in me. I had a knack for reading, and they constantly fed my learning appetite and encouraged me. I tested to go to the college preparatory magnet school, Summit High School, and I was accepted. From my first day of school at Summit, I felt like I belonged, at least academically. When I hopped the bus each day, it was like being transported to a new world and new home. It was magical. Unfortunately, I had to return to my house each day. Five times a week during the school year, I would be jerked back and forth between this high and low. Admittedly, I had a difficult time dealing with these swings. There were times when I actually had panic attacks on my way home. With the help of a few great teachers, a few wonderful friends, and Milo, I had survived my eighth and ninth grades and hoped to survive the tenth. As I walked home that night, I wondered how I would even survive the next few days much less the rest of this year and the two more years beyond that.

My pace slowed as I approached my house. I walked by my work place, Manny's Cactus Stop, with its large sign on the front. The sign had a picture of a guy wearing a sombrero sticking a faucet of some kind into a barrel cactus next to the words "Come In – Fill Up – Soda & Gas". At one end of the sign, the words were written in English while, at the other end, they were in Spanish. I hated the sign. It seemed cheesy.

My work at Manny's involved stocking shelves and cleaning up. I saw Manny inside with some customers and was tempted to stop, but I resisted and walked on. Manny paid me for five hours a week and was to pay me $8.00 an hour. The $40 a week had become my only source of funds. It's what I lived on. I couldn't remember the last time I had gotten money from my mom. Manny was a nice guy and easy to work for, but he was a cheapskate and he would often take advantage of me. On nearly every day I worked, he would keep me for twenty or thirty minutes longer than an hour, but he would only pay me for an hour. Early on with the job, I made sure to pick up a large bag of nuts and a drink to even the score a bit, but in the past year, I stopped that practice. I didn't think Manny would ever catch on, but any risk of getting caught and getting kicked out of school was too much for me. I never complained about his habit of shortchanging me because his pay was a lifeline for me. Still, I certainly didn't want to voluntarily drop by that evening. He could put me to work and not pay me at all. I moved on.

With no good alternative available, I arrived at my house. I stood still in front of the place and took a few minutes to study the old, three storied, brick apartment building. Before daring an entry, I circled around the outside of the building to take stock and make a better guess about the kind of atmosphere I might be walking into. I had done this in the past, and I certainly knew that it would be smart that evening. My first step would be to scout out the parking area in the back yard, off the alley, to see if JJ's old car was there in its usual spot. If the car wasn't there, I could probably get in without any big confrontation and retreat to my room. Then, if necessary, I could escape to the vacant third floor apartment via the old fire escape when JJ arrived. If his car was parked out back, I'd listen for any loud voices coming from the second floor, and depending upon what was being said, I'd decide the risk level. Since it was Friday night, I assumed they'd be at Cisco's.

I circled the house, found no car, and heard nothing that would raise my alarm. I eased up the back iron stairs that also served as the fire escape. I entered the enclosed, windowed porch, looked into the kitchen, and saw nothing but an empty plate setting near an open jar of peanut butter. I peered farther through the narrow kitchen and into the living room that had a nook where the television sat. I could tell from the moving shadows in the room that the television was on. Good. My twelve-year-old sister, who was called Little Maria after Mom, was the only one home. She'd been eating the only food that was usually available to either of us. When we were alone together, we teased each other and called ourselves the "peanut butter kids". Those times were some of the few when we connected in any way. We were just different from each other and typically went our separate ways. She never seemed to wonder about anything in life. She also never seemed to face being tormented by JJ. At least not in the way he treated me.

I left my backpack on our porch next to the old washer with a plan to immediately return and put in one small load of laundry. I needed to re-stock my survival pack. The apartment porches had never been intended as laundry areas, but they were the only places available in the old apartment building. The arrangement worked well as long as the water was turned off after each use in the winter. Otherwise, the pipes would break and the building owner would raise hell.

I was glad the apartment had a washer and dryer, and I had easily taught myself how to operate both. Doing my own gave me a feeling of independence and made it easier when I needed to escape. Even though those machines were available, I sometimes chose to use the ones at Lupe's Laundromat just to get away from the apartment when JJ was on the prowl. It was four blocks to the north of Manny's, and it was open all night. I had even slept on one of the folding tables a couple of times. I considered it to be one of my escape options.

As I hurried through the kitchen I saw Little Maria stick her head around the wall as she leaned back in a chair. "Oh, hi, Bucky. Mom said she wasn't sure you'd be back tonight and was really ragging on you. What's up?"

"Oh, I really can't explain it. JJ is always pissed at me and I think Mom is just taking his side. I'm not sure either one of them want me around, so I'm going to get some wash done, grab some food and a book, and lay low in my room."

Without showing any emotion, she responded with, "Oh, Okay," and immediately turned around to watch television while she grabbed a potato chip out of a bowl on a table next to her chair.

I had encountered longer conversations and more emotion with strangers on a bus than this brief interchange with my sister, but I wasn't upset. I figured out long ago that her survival method was to keep everyone at a distance and avoid connections. I supposed her approach was the less connected, the less hurt. With me, the disconnect method wouldn't work nor would it have been allowed to work with JJ on my back. For some reason, I was his favorite target. For Little Maria, though, her method seemed to work, and in the end, I pretty much ignored Sis as much as she ignored me.

That evening, I couldn't take time to linger on emotional analysis. Besides, there had been enough of that for one day, so I headed back through the kitchen and returned to the porch. I unloaded a few dirty items from the backpack, took it to my room, and retrieved some other dirty clothes. Backtracking, I tossed the items in as the washer filled. Almost each item of clothing that I owned was dark colored. This allowed me to get by with only one load, at least most of the time. With each visit to the Goodwill Store, I made sure to keep that in mind. Easy access, single loads, and self-sufficiency weren't just laundry skills; they helped me survive.

The apartment building was narrow and had an old-style layout. Each of the three apartments in this building followed the same floor plan. The layout went from the back porch to the galley-type kitchen, living room, and the front door. The front entry led to a large concrete porch with white columns and a wide, concrete staircase. This was originally designed to be the main entrance and a place to sit out, but, with parking in the back, it was now used for storage. The living room had a bay window on the outside wall and a five-foot opening on the other side that allowed entry into a small hall area that had three doorways immediately off of that opening. This was the primary access point to the opposite side of the apartment. One doorway led to the main bedroom that looked out onto the front porch, the door in the middle was to the only restroom, and the third went to a tiny bedroom that Little Maria occupied.

Little Maria's bedroom had a second door on the opposite end that led to my bedroom. My bed blocked the shared door so it was never used. Luckily, my room had a second door as well. It led to the kitchen and was right next to the back porch entry. That door had a lock, and I used it. My room also had a window that opened to the back porch. The window was another escape route. Except to use the toilet, I was seldom found on the front side of the apartment. In fact, I even tried to limit my use of the restroom. I took opportunities to shower at school, used Manny's restroom on workdays, and dropped by McDonald's after my bus dropped me off. I even took a whiz in the weeds by the homeless camp on occasion. I kept track of my options and knew how to take advantage of them.

Although I allowed my mind to wander when I was locked in my room or completely away from the apartment, I found myself to be very focused when doing something in the apartment outside my room. That territory carried a risk and I felt vulnerable. I had a sense that a timer was going to go off any minute and interrupt my progress and wellbeing. With that focus, I went in and out of my room and tried to concentrate while, at the same time, I listened to the alarm clock in my head. My next step was to grab some food to re-stock Big Red. The one cabinet shelf that held the few food items available was nearly empty, so I tried to pick items that might not be missed. I took a can of tuna, one little bag of chips, one bag of crackers from the larger cracker box to go with my ever-ready supply of peanut butter, and one can of pork and beans. It may not have made for the breakfast of champions, but it would certainly do as a snack for a survivor.

After stashing the food items and eating a PB&J sandwich, I looked through all the mail to make sure there was nothing related to me, especially from the school. As I went to the back porch to get the dry laundry, I heard a car drive up and saw the lights as it pulled onto the gravel, mud, and grass parking area behind the house. I could tell by the loud muffler that it was JJ's car. I heard two doors slam and two yelling voices; I knew it was my mom and JJ. They were arguing.

I hurriedly took my stuff to my room and locked the door, but I remembered that I had forgotten to shut off the water valve to the washer. I tried to rush back to the porch, turn the water off, and beat it back to my room before they made it to the top of the rickety old iron stairs, but no such luck. Just as I finished turning off the valve, JJ opened the porch door, hesitated for a second, and gave me a hateful look. As he looked at me and as I stood backed into a corner, I noticed a streak of blood on his shirt, a drip of blood coming out his left nostril, and a busted lip. He said nothing, turned into the kitchen, stomped across the floor and disappeared toward the restroom.

My mom was right on JJ's heels. She had a bruise and some swelling under her left eye and a scratched face. Both of them smelled of booze. Mom lowered her head as if to cover up her face and said, "So, they let you come home, huh?" Her tone seemed a mix of disappointment and embarrassment. I couldn't sort it out or respond. How could I have said anything that would have made sense of that scene or even made much sense of that day? Unfortunately, what would have been an exceptionally rare day of craziness for most people was but a new verse to an old song for me.

I wanted to stare a hole right through her. Finally, Mom sighed, turned away from me, and shuffled and stumbled inside without me responding to the question. I went to my room, picked up a sock that I had dropped, locked my door and hoped that JJ didn't come back my way. I picked up a book and tried to melt into the story, but I was so spent that for once, I couldn't even read. I just stared at the wall, listened for danger, and tried to think of any way to ease the deep feelings of hurt that were crushing me from the inside out. I was glad that JJ had gotten a taste of his own medicine, but that did nothing to soothe my storm of thoughts and feelings. As I sat on my bed and looked around the closet-like room, I realized that it was much smaller than Milo's tent. I wondered who was better off and wished that I had Milo as my sentry.

I was prepared to make a hasty retreat up the broken fire escape to the vacant third floor, but eventually the activity outside my door ended and the lights went off. I was actually able to sleep in my own bed that night.

CHAPTER SIX
The Theory of Friends

I woke up in a jolt thinking that something was wrong, but I could hear only a slight, occasional snapping or clipping sound coming from somewhere outside my door. I didn't recognize the sound, but it didn't seem to pose any danger. For some reason, I had slept well. I must have been exhausted. I looked at my clock and was glad the sound had awakened me. It was 7:30. I realized that I had forgotten to set the alarm, and that I had only thirty minutes before I had to be at Manny's. I knew I could make that easily. Occasionally, on Saturdays, Manny wanted me for two hours, and today was one of those days. I was glad for the extra hour of work as it would give me an extra $8.00 and it would help to keep my mind off of Harper's health crisis.

With a habitual, easy move, I jumped into my black sweatshirt and jeans, pulled my socks and heavy boots on, grabbed Big Red, and stepped out of my room. As I exited, I noticed my mom sitting on a stool leaning over a portion of the kitchen counter. Next to her on the counter was an array of repulsive items including a full ashtray, some empty cans, and a dirty rag. All of this was normal…gross, but normal. She had a cigarette in her mouth and a cup of coffee beside her. This too was normal. The only thing out of the ordinary was the fact that she was in the midst of clipping her long, dirty, red fingernails.

I stood at the doorway ready to exit through the back porch, but was looking at her wondering why she was clipping her long nails down to the nub.

I thought she liked long nails. She finally looked up, took a long drag on the cigarette, and blew out a cloud of smoke. Without me even asking a question, she coughed and spoke in her raspy voice. "Well, if you must know, I broke a couple of 'em last night at Cisco's while I was scratching the eyes out of Tina."

"I didn't say a thing."

"Oh, you did too. I know that look." Then she laughed and, seemingly with pride, she continued. "I was getting the best of that hussy until Teddy, her guy, stepped in and shoved me off her. Then, the most romantic thing happened. JJ jumped on Teddy. First time a man has ever tried to protect me. In the end, JJ got the crap beat out of him, but still, it was a great thing to watch. We all kind of made up at the end. Of course, JJ had his pride hurt. So after a few more beers, we just headed home. What a night." She looked down and continued to clip those dirty nails with the cut ends flying all over the kitchen. The last one hit a dusty, old crucifix sitting on the window ledge over the kitchen sink.

The whole scene left me speechless. I thought to myself, "This life is getting the best of me," but, again, I couldn't verbalize anything, clever or not. That was the second day in a row I had felt dumbfounded. As I was shaking my head and feeling a headache coming on from either the smoke or my mom's words, I mumbled and I headed out the door, "Gotta' go to work. See you later." I lied. I hadn't planned on seeing her later, if I could help it. As I carefully descended the shaky fire escape and walked towards Manny's, I realized that in that brief, morning encounter, Mom's comments pretty much said it all about her life. I also realized that she had not asked one thing or said one word about my appointment with the shrink the day before. I could only wonder why.

My plan was to finish my work at Manny's by the end of the two hours and not let him talk me into staying even a few minutes extra. I wanted to take the bus to Corina Schuler's house. She would know if Harper's surgery was on for Monday. I also wanted to find out if Corina was going to get out of school that Monday and go over to the hospital. If she was going, I wanted to go with her, especially if one of her parents was planning to take her over. I thought I could hook up with them, save my bus money, and beat the weather, if it was bad. If I got back soon enough in the afternoon, I'd drop by Milo's.

The work at Manny's went quickly and all went well. I filled all the drink coolers with what must have been fifty different kinds of drinks. I stocked the shelves with candy, chips, motor oil, magazines, and twenty to thirty other items. Plus, I went outside and filled up the paper towel dispensers by the gas pumps. The only things I didn't handle were the personal items in the restrooms. Manny was in a great mood. Business had been good and he hadn't been burglarized or robbed in almost a year. He even let me take a break and eat two big burritos without deducting the cost out of my pay.

While I was eating, Manny asked me in broken English, "Hey, what's wrong with you today? You haven't asked me one question. You always ask questions. Are you thinking about that pretty girl of yours?"

Usually, I talked very little about my personal life with Manny, and usually, Manny didn't seem to want to know much. For some reason, however, I allowed a few thoughts to spill out. "I definitely think of her as my pretty girlfriend. On the other hand, I'm not sure she thinks she's my girl. Yes, I'm thinking about her and worried about her. She has to have open-heart surgery probably on Monday. It sure seems serious to me. By the way, do you mind if I don't come in Monday? I could come in Sunday evening for an hour. I'm going to try to be at the hospital on Monday and really don't know if I can get back here by 4:00 like usual."

Manny's face went pale and he responded to my news by hurriedly crossing himself. Although Manny didn't go to Mass, he never failed to tell people that he was a good Catholic and crossed himself when he thought it appropriate. I was never sure what standards he used to decide that, but obviously Harper's surgery had risen to the occasion. He followed his speedy, superstitious-like hand movement with a quick, "Oh, bless you. Jesus be with her." After spitting this out, he immediately walked away and found a customer with an offer to help them.

Talking about God and religion didn't bother me much, but I just couldn't seem to find a place to fit God or religion into a logical mindset, especially the way Manny expressed it. I often wondered about God, and even tried to start reading the Bible a few times, but my wondering always seemed to reach a dead end, so that was one subject that I just pretty much left alone. I had taken a position that said that I didn't believe in God, but the truth was that I simply didn't feel like I had any way to know about things like that. I had enough trouble dealing with the things that I did see. I knew that Harper and Corina's parents were believers, but I hadn't felt the need to ask them why they believed or exactly what they believed. I certainly couldn't imagine that they thought about God in the same way as Manny.

As work ended, Manny handed me a twenty dollar bill and told me that he was giving me a little extra that day saying, "You do good work today." Again, with the money delivered, he scurried off to do something else. It was clear that he cared, but also just as clear that he was not one to sit and talk or listen. He was a man of many words, but with those words, he made every effort to stay at the surface. He was one more person in my life who thought my wondering and asking was odd. He would say, "I give you friendly advice. You keep turning rocks, you someday find tarantula." When he would say that, I would always come back with something like, "Well, I won't ever find gold unless I look." He would then seriously wag his finger as though he was issuing a warning.

I wrapped up my duties, hung up my work apron, cleaned up in the rest room, put on my coat, and went into the cooler to grab my backpack. The cooler was the best place for it as the big thing was out of the way and the cooler seemed to be the most secure location. Just in case, I checked several of the zippered pockets that held my most valued items and threw it in a wide half-circle allowing it to land on my back as I tucked my arms into the main straps. Once on and balanced, it became part of me.

Going out the door, I said "Hello, friend," to River Ralph, a guy I knew from Milo's camp. He smiled in return and gave me a short wave of the hand. Manny saw the exchange and shook his head. Occasionally, Manny had asked me why I talked to "those disgusting guys" from the camp. Outside, I saw a lady filling up her car with gas and greeted her in the same manner as I had River Ralph. She was a regular customer and had always seemed friendly. Her response was a happy greeting back to me, and she asked how I was doing. Even though I only knew these people through contact at Manny's or the homeless camp, I felt they were as close to adult friends as I was probably ever going to have. I hadn't known other adults through family like most kids. Plus, the other adults, who I did know, were parents of kids at school or teachers. There was Dr. Guss from yesterday, but he fit the same kind of role. They were all great and nice, but none seemed like they were my friends first. They had their jobs to do, and I felt that I had only a second place position with them. So, whether it was pretending or not, I would think of these people as friends. Of course, it was my special relationship with Harper that was most on my mind. There could be no substitute for her.

I took a shortcut down an alley and headed towards Lupe's Laundromat to use one of the few pay phones still around. I could have used the phone at Manny's, but I decided not to. I didn't want him listening in and asking what was going on. I didn't want to talk to him. I wanted to talk to Corina.

I called Corina's cell number and asked her if she minded me dropping by to talk about Harper. She welcomed my call and said that it would be great if I came by. She seemed to want to talk as much as I did. She just finished soccer practice and would be home in about 45 minutes. I hung up, jogged back towards 7th and Shawnee, and checked the bus schedule at the stop in front of McDonald's. I still had a 30-minute wait. I took advantage of the delay by going into McDonald's and ordered a cup of coffee. I really didn't like coffee that much, but some of my friends drank it and it was warm. Besides, it let me hang out inside to wait for the bus. I grabbed a window seat that allowed me to see the bus coming from five blocks away. It came over the Prairie River Bridge right on time.

The bus took me to the intersection of 18th and Grand Street, near St. Paul's. St. Paul's Cathedral, high school, and elementary school sat side by side on this one block square site. I remembered that Corina had attended that elementary school until 7th grade. Like me, she had tested into Summit High School and enrolled in Summit beginning in the 8th grade. She sometimes talked about some of her friends who didn't transfer and who attended St. Paul's High School. Corina's home was only three blocks to the east in this older, but very well kept neighborhood. Thirty years ago, before suburban development, this was considered one of the nicest parts of Freeman City. I still considered it a great neighborhood. I marveled at the beautiful, three-story homes with the nicely landscaped lawns. This neighborhood wasn't off the charts like Harper's Indian Heights section of town, just twelve blocks north, but it was way above anything Armourvale had to offer.

THE SECRETS OF CUTTING GRASS

I quickly walked the three blocks to Corina's home, rang the bell, and soon heard someone running to the door. By the sound of the footsteps, it was either Corina or her brother, Mark. Corina opened the door with a big smile and greeted me with a hug. Unlike Harper, she had no reservations about a full out hug. Of course, we had no current crush going on either, although it would be easy to get used to being around her. Corina was smart and pretty like Harper, but they really didn't look anything alike. She had reddish brown hair, creamy white skin, green eyes, and an athletic build. She was the only girl on the boy's soccer team, because Summit had no girl's team. She could outrun many of the guys and wasn't afraid of mixing it up. It hadn't been unusual to see her come to school with injuries, but I never heard about her missing practice.

Finishing our hug, she quickly started giving me instructions in her fast-paced chatter and with her hands flying in all directions that had no relationship to the instructions being given. "Come into the kitchen and sit down. Here sit over here. We're having a snack, what do you want? We have two kinds of chips, soda or milk, and Mom has some double chocolate brownies coming out of the oven. Do you want a dip of ice cream on your brownie?"

I said, "Sure," which led everyone around, including her mom, to erupt in loud laughter.

"Sorry, Buck, but what are you saying sure to?" her mom asked.

"Oh, yeah. Well, I'll have a Dr. Pepper and some Doritos for now, but would love to have a brownie with ice cream when it's ready. I can't think of the last time I had a hot brownie with ice cream. That sounds great."

"Well, that's exactly what you'll get. It's so nice to have someone so appreciative of my work, Buck," said Mrs. Schuler. Even though we all knew that this was a difficult time and that we would need to talk about Harper's situation at some point, the Schuler's friendly atmosphere made it okay to have a good time, even if we were getting together to share our worries.

Over the past two years, I had visited the Schuler's home several times and I loved each visit. They seemed to love loud talk. They even liked to argue, but seemed to do so without getting mad. It wouldn't be unusual to see things like Corina wrestle her brother on the floor or Corina's dad, who was called Chip, pick up Mrs. Schuler and swirl her around or the whole family erupt in a popcorn fight. Mr. Schuler blamed the noise level on Mrs. Schuler. He would say that it was all because of her red hair and Irish background. She would usually respond to that by throwing something at him. I knew they loved the outdoors, but sometimes it seemed liked they brought the outdoor activities to the indoors. In many ways the Schuler family was a different animal than the Hawkins family.

The Hawkins' household looked and even sounded much differently than the Schuler's. It was much more reserved. Except for their pool time in the summer, they enjoyed the fine arts more than the outdoors. Mrs. Hawkins also loved to travel, especially to Paris. Reading was their passion. Interestingly, I loved being around both families. Each had some kind of common glue that created a bond that I knew was special, but I wasn't able to define exactly what it was.

Corina and I sat at the large, round table that occupied the corner of this large open kitchen that looked brand new. Her Mom and her brother joined us. We munched and talked about lots of fun stuff including that day's soccer practice, a movie that Corina had seen, and about how well her brother, Mark, had done on a math test. Considering my insane family life, it was weird for me to see the Schuler family having fun with each other. They teased, gave high fives, and shoved one another when saying things like "shut-up" with a laugh. Corina even gave her mom an intentional shoulder slap as she walked by her once while getting her phone. Her mom responded with, "Watch it!" and pretended to be angry.

It was also fun to reminisce with Corina about the first time we met. I met her at the exact same time I met Harper. We were assigned to the same Biology class at Summit, and during the first week of classes, the teacher broke the class into small groups with an assignment to create a game that would give students a creative way to learn science facts. Harper, Corina, and I were put in the same group of five. The three of us dominated the discussion, teased each other, and left the other two classmates in the dust. I was amazed at the intelligence, verbal skills, and creativeness of Corina and Harper, but was especially smitten by the way Harper kept looking at me.

Our game was not only judged the best from the groups, but Mr. Stinson, our teacher, eventually sent the game into a state contest. We only received a letter of recognition and not an award, but we still thought it was cool. Corina and I remembered the game like it was yesterday. We called it "Seven Facts/Seven Sames", and it involved creating seven facts about any object or substance in the world that would allow someone to distinguish it from any other. It was a take off of the game Twenty Questions. One player would create the seven facts and another would try to identify the object with the fewest number of facts given. If the player wasn't successful after seven facts were given, the player was given ten penalty points on top of the seven. After five rounds, the player with the lowest score would win. There was also a wild card way to win immediately. That required a player to come up with seven facts about two separate elements that were exactly the same. No one ever did that, but Harper came close one day.

Harper loved to play games but said that neither of her parents enjoyed games. In fact, her dad refused to play games at all. Because of this, she constantly bugged me to play Scrabble with her at lunch. We enjoyed it so much that we evented our own form of Scrabble called Flash Scrabble. We placed a magnetic board with magnetic letters onto the end of a metal bookcase located in the library near an out-of-the-way corner. Whenever we passed by the library, we would rush in and make a play within seconds and rush out. We played five or six games over a two-week period before we were put out of business. One day, Harper and Corina rushed in to make a play, but the board was missing and only a few letters remained on the metal cabinet. The letters spelled out "game over" with the letter "e" being the shared letter. We had been busted, but in a nice way.

As we laughed over that story, the brownies were delivered with the promised ice cream. Our talk was silenced for about five minutes. All you could hear was "Mmm."

When the bowls were empty, everyone got up with their bowl. I wondered what was happening, but soon followed suit and took my bowl to the dishwasher. Mrs. Schuler said, "Why thank you, Buck, but you didn't need to do that, you're a guest here."

"Ma'am, I'll do that every day if I can have that kind of food."

She took me by the shoulders, and said, "Well, in that case, I may just have to have you stay for supper. Now, I know you and Corina want to talk about Elise, and I'm going to chase Mark off so that we can talk, but I'm going to sit in for a bit just to see how Chip and I, I mean, how Mr. Schuler and I can best help out. I hope you don't mind, but this is emotional for all of us and we need to be a part of this."

I didn't mind at all, but I looked to Corina to judge her feelings. She had her lips pressed together which seemed either a bit negative or that she was just taking it all in. Slowly, she started nodding her head up and down and relaxed her lips so I knew this was going to be fine. Then she got up out of her chair from my side of the table and went over by her mom, sat next to her, and leaned her head into her mom.

Corina looked up at her mom with tears coming out of her eyes and said, "Mom, I'm just so scared for Ellie. I just can't imagine what she's thinking. If I had to think about someone cutting my chest open and touching my heart, I would go bonkers. I know that she might die without this operation, but I don't know what I'd do if she died in the operating room."

"I know. I'm heartsick over this too," said Mrs. Schuler. She looked at me and asked me, "How are you taking this, Buck?"

I was caught for a moment as I wondered if Mrs. Schuler was even aware of her use of the word, "heartsick", but I quickly re-focused and spoke slowly. "You know I call her Harper. Mainly, I wanted to find out if the surgery is on or not for Monday, but I can tell by the comments it's set to go." I listened to my own words and the reality of the situation gave me a heavy feeling.

I took a moment to catch my breath and tried to hold onto my emotions before I allowed any other words to leak out. "My feelings are like Corina's, and I feel alone with all of this."

My feelings were actually all over the place, but I wanted to skip right to the practical matter most on my mind. "Most of all, though, I'd sure like to ride over to the hospital with you all on Monday and sit with you. "

Mrs. Schuler readily agreed to pick me up and give me a ride. With that settled I felt more like talking. The three of us shared our worries for the next hour. For some reason, I trusted them and they listened with care. I can't say that I felt good at the end about Harper's health, but I certainly felt less alone, like we were in this together. We worked out the details for Mrs. Schuler and Corina to pick me up at McDonald's at 6:00 a.m. on Monday morning. We needed to be at the hospital by 7:00 if we wanted to say hello. I was glad Corina's mom hadn't used the word goodbye. I asked for one more favor from Corina and her mom. I asked if I could use one of their phones to call Harper. I explained that I just couldn't bring myself to go to the Hawkins' house the next day, as I felt that I would just add to Harper's emotions. On the other hand, I at least wanted to talk to her over the phone.

Mrs. Schuler jumped up and said, "Why didn't I think of that. Buck, that's exactly what you should do." She went into another room, brought out a phone, showed me into a windowed porch, and told me to take as long as I wanted. I talked to Harper for an hour and had a soaked sleeve when I finished. Still, I felt that it had gone well. Harper amazed me. For some reason, she seemed to be more at peace over this than I was. I could tell that her parents were in the same room with her, but she was still able to make personal comments about how much I meant to her. I wasn't sure what the concept or experience of love fully meant, but I felt something for her that was on a different level than I thought was possible. Of course, in some ways, it made me even more afraid. The thought of losing the best thing in my life was terrifying.

When I was done with the call to Harper, I made one more quick call to my school counselor, Mrs. Sheppard. Mrs. Sheppard knew all about my home life and had given me her home number in case of a crisis. She had told me that I was a special student and that I shouldn't let something come up that would screw up my record. I kept that phone number as a valued possession in my billfold. It had become a symbol that at least one adult cared about me. The piece of paper with the number on it had become crumpled and discolored, but it was still in the spot where I had put it. Luckily, she was home and greeted me as though I was her best friend. She readily agreed to call my mom on Monday so that my absence would be considered properly excused. I told her that my mom didn't know about Harper's surgery and that she would have to do some explaining. Mrs. Sheppard also knew about my special relationship with Harper. She thought Harper was special, too, and was upset by the news. She reassured me that she would handle it and that my teachers would be given updates.

When I finished my calls and came back into the dining area next to the kitchen. Mrs. Schuler noticed my red eyes and gave me a rough hug.

I wasn't much of a hugger, but it was a common practice in their house to give less than gentle hugs. It seemed the more something meant, the rougher the hug. With that round of hugging done, she made it clear that I was in fact invited to dinner. It was an easy call. I stayed and decided that my visit to Milo would have to wait another day. The meal was as good as any I could have ever even dreamed about, even though to them it was simple. Mrs. Schuler fixed homemade rolls, meatloaf, mashed potatoes and gravy, and topped the meal off with peach cobbler and ice cream. I didn't want to leave, but when Mr. Schuler got home from his Saturday shift at his utility company, he said that he would give me a ride, but only if he could take me before he showered. "I want to eat and relax after I shower. Does that work for you?" As if to emphasize his point, he smiled and slapped me on the back.

I laughed and agreed, "Yeah, I need to get out of here before I get too many bruises from the hugs and backslaps." Of course, that prompted a final round of hugs. I crawled into Chip's pickup and was soon back at the corner of 7th and Shawnee. Mr. Schuler gave me a final slap on the shoulder, said "see you later", and gunned the truck up the road.

As Mr. Schuler headed back to his world and as I reoriented to mine, I decided that my view of adult friends needed revision. Just because some had other significant roles didn't mean for certain that a few couldn't become important friends.

CHAPTER SEVEN
Fingernails

Most of Sunday was a blur with few memories. It had snowed several inches overnight, so I decided to again delay my visit to Milo. I really wanted to talk to him, but I wasn't as desperate to do so since visiting with the Schuler family and after talking to Harper yesterday. With Milo off my to-do-list, I stayed in my room almost the entire day. I used the time to read and I worked ahead on homework. I only ventured out when I saw JJ outside messing with his car or when he ran an errand. An errand for him probably involved picking up a six-pack.

For some reason, the most significant memory of that day involved the gross debris lying around the kitchen. Even though I only ventured out of my room a few times, each exit took me into the kitchen, and each time in the kitchen I faced my mom's discarded, dirty, red fingernails still lying where they had randomly fallen on Saturday morning. Each time I saw the dead ends, I was not only grossed out by the nails, but I was bothered by the thought of what, or maybe who, they represented. I faced the choice of two worlds that day. Stay in my cell or step out and look at the other reality in my life. I knew from Harper that Sunday was supposed to be a day of rest, but for me it had been just another exhausting day of confinement and depression. By the end of the day, even with no physical exertion, I felt weary.

My thinking and worrying nagged at me into that Sunday night. Because of that, I didn't sleep well. In spite of a lack of sleep, I was ready and waiting when Mrs. Schuler and Corina pulled into McDonald's. Corina had told her mom that I would be on time and teased me. She said that I had OCD like she did, only worse. She also teased me about McDonald's; she thought the restaurant was my true home. I laughed at both comments, especially since both had elements of truth. Even as they teased me, they made me feel special. Being around them led me to the conclusion that good-natured teasing was really a sign of acceptance and friendship. I wished that I could figure out a proper way to say thanks for what Mrs. Schuler and Corina were doing, but too much else was happening for me to give much attention to that for now.

Although the streets were slick, the Schuler's nice SUV navigated the snowy distance with no difficulty as we made our short trek to the hospital. Corina and I sat in the back seat. She reached across the bucket seats to squeeze my hand. It was her method of comforting both of us, and it seemed to work better than talking.

When we got to the Med Center, we traipsed through the cold, concrete parking garage and into the lobby where I had been just that last Friday. We rode the escalators up one floor and then hopped onto an elevator to the fourth floor and found our way to a surgical waiting area. We had been told to meet Mr. and Mrs. Hawkins in this specific area before we would be allowed to have a brief visit with Harper. As we got off the elevator in this new section of the hospital, I thought of the irony of the psych unit being on the same floor even though it was in the old section of the hospital. I looked around for windows to see if I could look over to the old building, and I saw only one. As I looked out of this single window, I could only see the dimly lit outline of the old building. The psych unit was out of sight.

Mr. and Mrs. Hawkins came out of the pre-op area within minutes of our arrival and hugs went all around. Mr. Hawkins shook my hand and gave me a gentle pat on the back. Both of Harper's parents told me how special it was for me to miss school and stay with them. Evidently, Harper had already asked about me. I asked how she was holding up and Mrs. Hawkins said, "Well, she thinks it's freezing in there and she's shaking like a leaf, but she's okay. She just keeps saying that by tomorrow, this will be over and she will be on the mend. We just keep telling ourselves the same thing, but we are still really worried. Buck, you just can't know what it's like to worry over a child like that. As a parent, each time she hurts,

Max and I would wish it were one of us, instead of her. I'm sure that's true with most parents. Harper is the best thing that has ever happened to us. We pray all the time for God to protect her."

I didn't know what to say to either of their comments on prayer or parents. I agreed that Harper was the best thing to ever happen to us, but I couldn't figure out how anything could exist to hear any prayer, because if there were a God, he surely wouldn't have allowed Harper's heart problem. As I was thinking all that, I just said, "Yes, she's the best."

When the time came, we all lined up to speak with Harper, but we were only allowed seconds to go in and out of the room. We went in two at a time. I went in with Max. For some reason, Mr. Hawkins asked me to call him Max. I assumed that I would have time to visit with Harper and to say something really important, but there wasn't much more to be said. I just whispered in her ear that she was the most special person in my life and that I would see her in a bit. She blew me a kiss and I backed up while Max said his words, and before I could think, I found myself sitting in a chair in the waiting room with gobs of other people.

Harper's mom and dad, two of their friends, Harper's aunt, a friend from Harper's church, Corina, Mrs. Schuler, and I sat in one alcove area while other families of other surgery patients clustered together in different sections that they had carved out. Patients were assigned numbers and occasionally information was to be listed on two large, overhead screens. I had only been in an airport once, but these overheads seemed to be similar to those screens listing arrival and departure times at the airport. At the front of the room was a desk with two volunteers with sheets of paper listing patients and who knows what else. Most people there seemed to have a robotic stare; with eyes constantly transfixed to one of the screens. Someone explained that this system was meant to protect patients' privacy, but it acted like an impersonal barrier. I knew that my special girl was just a few yards from me, but I felt helplessly separated.

The Hawkins' minister had dropped in and said a prayer. Harper's Aunt Beth kept up a dialogue as she sat next to Mrs. Hawkins, and a good friend of Mr. Hawkins, Larry, sat next to him.

I sat with Corina and Mrs. Schuler in chairs opposite from Mrs. Hawkins. As we visited, Corina's mom asked me to call her Del. She said, "My friends don't call me Mrs. Schuler or Deloris, and since we're going to be spending some time together today, calling me Del will make me feel more comfortable."

At one point as we waited, Mrs. Hawkins came over to give Corina and me extra attention. She also gave us a little more information on the surgery and the estimated time that it could take. It should take anywhere from three to four hours, but we will likely get an update before then. Both Mrs. Hawkins and Mrs. Schuler encouraged me to go to the cafeteria with Corina just to break up the time. One of them would call us on Corina's phone if anything happened. We agreed. While in the cafeteria, I insisted on sitting where Harper and I had visited just that previous Friday night. I shared my memories of that evening with Corina who was again squeezing my hand.

After an hour, Corina and I came back up to the cardiac center's surgical waiting area and pretended to read outdated magazines. Three hours passed. I wondered out loud, "Why haven't we gotten an update?"

Harper's mom, Lucie, quickly said, "I agree. I feel like I'm barely hanging on by my fingernails."

Finally, Harper's number had information scrolling across the board. The screen indicated that Harper's surgery was in progress and that she should be moved to recovery within the next hour. I thought to myself "duh", that's not very helpful. Within the next thirty minutes, several other patient screens indicated "Out of Surgery - In Recovery", but Harper's screen retained the old information. If those screens had been intended to reduce anxiety, they seemed to have done just the opposite for our group. Finally the message had changed, but instead of the expected "In Recovery", it had a message for Harper's parents to report to room "A" for an update. Room "A" was a small conference room off the main waiting room. Mr. and Mrs. Hawkins hurried in and waited. A tall man with surgical scrubs entered the same room and closed the door. The meeting probably only lasted five minutes, but I and the others left waiting in the main waiting area didn't move the whole time. We sat like frozen statues while we stared at the door to that little conference room. Other families in the waiting area looked at us with concern or, maybe, pity. Either way, we didn't care. We just wanted to know. My fear and anxiety levels were maxed out and I felt like at any second I might puke.

The door opened. The surgeon left. The Hawkins returned to their chairs with ashen faces, pulled their chairs up close to ours and gave us the bad news. Mr. and Mrs. Hawkins didn't use the phrase "bad news", but used the phrase, "There is a bit of a concern." The doctors indicated that during the surgery all had looked great. Harper had gone on and off the bypass machine without difficulty. Also, the heart repair had gone quite smoothly, and that she had, in fact, been moved to recovery. For some reason, however, they were having difficulty getting her to wake up, and that had prompted them to leave her on the breathing machine, which she called the ventilator. I had no idea what this meant or why this was a concern.

I wondered if it was a "bit of a concern" or really a "big damn crisis". I just couldn't tell. I don't think Mrs. Hawkins knew for sure either. As Mrs. Hawkins shared, Mr. Hawkins sat rigid with eyes down, and this made me wonder all the more. Mrs. Hawkins was teary eyed as she talked, but that wasn't unusual. She often referred to herself as a crier, and she actually seemed more able to speak than he did. She went on to give as much of the information as she could and seemed to be trying to give it almost verbatim from how the doctor had shared it.

As Mrs. Hawkins continued, several of the other ladies started sniffling, but, for the most part, the group was reserved. I wanted to jump up and yell, "So what does this mean?" Instead, I tried to act like the adults.

Mrs. Hawkins, who knew the medical language, went on, "Well, as I was saying, Dr. Alexander, the surgeon, wanted to take her off the vent, but, because she's not waking up, he wants to keep her in recovery for a little bit to see what's going on. He said one of the potential complications with these kinds of operations is that when they put her on the bypass machine, they use a blood thinner to keep from having blood clots, but with some patients, this thinner can lead to a bleed in the brain that, in turn, could cause a mild stroke. He's going to keep an eye on this for a bit before he sends her up to the ICU. He seemed to be preparing us to see her still on the vent when she got to ICU." She looked to Max to confirm her understanding and her wording. "Did I get that right, Honey?"

Max responded with a slight sigh and a nodding of the head, "That's exactly the way I understood it. Yes, the doctor seemed a bit worried. I think you about covered it all. The only other thing is that someone would be out again in just a little bit and give us another update."

I thought to myself, well if he's worried then I'm scared to death, and that information from the doctor doesn't cover it all for me. I wanted to know, "Is she going to be all right?" I also thought the words "in a little bit" in a hospital don't mean the same thing as "in a little bit" in school or at Manny's. The hospital needs a different phrase. I thought "in a little bit" probably really means they have no idea.

Mrs. Hawkins then jumped back into the conversation with a start, "Oh! Oh! I forgot to share something else the surgeon said that I thought was, well, odd, but special. Even if it was odd, I'm going to take it as a God thing. In that very room, he looked at me and told me to keep hanging on, even if it was hanging on by my fingernails, and that we would all get through this. He said we just need a little more time to sort this out. Now, there is no way he could have known that I had just said that almost exact same thing just an hour or so ago! So, I just know that she's going to be all right. What do you think of that?" Mr. Hawkins looked at her with a shake of his head, but he let out a smile nonetheless.

Before we could respond, Mrs. Hawkins picked up her narrative again with, "Now, if we are going to all hang on by our fingernails, then we need to do it right."

I had no idea what she meant, especially when she said the words "if we." I had thought the doctor was telling her. But the more she talked, the more she seemed to gain strength and focus and she started to dig around in her massive purse hunting for something.

From my point of view, I was feeling like I had been clubbed with a sledgehammer. I couldn't for the life of me find any good in any of the facts that I had heard. I heard the word "stroke", and I nearly choked. I couldn't seem to swallow my own spit. I tried to bring my hands up to my mouth, but couldn't move my left hand. I finally realized that Corina had squeezed it so tightly that it had seemed to merge with her hand and that her hand was fixed to the chair.

Nothing felt or sounded at all good to me, and I was about to panic. As I stewed with worry, Mrs. Hawkins yelled out, "Eureka" as she found what she was looking for: her cell phone. She hurriedly punched a couple of buttons and proceeded to make a call to one of her best friends, Mrs. Sorenzen. When Mrs. Sorenzen answered, an odd conversation ensued. Mrs. Hawkins said, "Joyce. Hi. This is Lucie. Would you mind doing me a favor? Good. Would you run by the store and pick up some purple and pink nail polish and bring it to the hospital as soon as possible? Well, she's not doing well, but I'll tell you more when you get here. Just don't forget the nail polish."

The brief conversation then ended. It was clear that Mrs. Sorenzen had agreed to bring the polish without even asking why, and I found that to be just as weird. Wouldn't any normal, sane person ask why? Instead, I could tell that Mrs. Sorenzen had only asked for directions to the ICU waiting room. I looked at Max for an interpretation, but he wasn't really tuned in to that. He seemed to be just holding his gut while looking at the floor. I had nothing to do and could only watch and listen. I wondered, is this what people normally do in hospital waiting rooms?

Mrs. Hawkins hung up the phone, looked at the group, and took a deep breath. She then said in announcement style, "Max and I and Ellie have had our prayer time about this and whatever happens we will get through it even if we do have to hang on by our nails. Besides our prayers, we had our time to talk, and we promised Harper." She then looked at me and went on with, "Buck, you've got me saying Harper. We promised Harper Elise that, no matter what, we would be with her every step of the way and that we would not give up or give in until the final chapter is written. We aim to keep that promise and we expect each of you to help with this. I've asked one of my friends to bring some nail polish so that I can polish Ellie's nails as soon as she is out of recovery and in ICU. If the doctor says for us to hang on by our fingernails then we are going to show him and show Ellie and show anyone who wants to know that we are in this together and committed to a full recovery. If we are going to be hanging on by our nails, by golly our nails are going to be pretty. When she wakes up, we are going to try to tell her what's up with her pretty nails. Ours included."

Finally we were notified that Harper was being moved from recovery to the ICU. Our group was preparing to move in that direction, as well. However, before the move, we received another update. That update came from Dr. Mills instead of the surgeon. She said that Harper had begun to come around. Even with that, they had decided to leave the vent in place. The information didn't really say much about how Harper was doing, but it was still helpful. Dr. Mills told us what they would be looking for to determine if there had been a mild stroke or some other issue. She also gave us a clear indication that the heart was doing great. With Dr. Mills' caring style, everyone seemed to have really appreciated her visit, and they especially liked the fact that she met with the whole group. This was probably easier to do because, by then, the surgery waiting area had almost emptied. I personally appreciated it because Dr. Mills had asked if anyone had any questions and I leaned in and asked, "Are you for certain that Harper will make it?"

Dr. Mills moved up on the front of her chair, smiled, and slowly, deliberately, and with confidence said, "Yes. I see no problem with saying yes to that. I'm hoping that she perks up here in the next couple of hours and that all will be good. I'm also hoping that in the next couple of days, she will be well enough to move her to another level of care like acute care, and gradually progress to a regular cardiac bed."

After that update and after another hour or so, Harper arrived in ICU. By then, our group was already in the waiting room for that unit.

Mrs. Sorenzen had no problem tracking us down. When she arrived, she stood for just a moment at the entry to the waiting area, loudly said "hello, everybody", and proceeded to look around the room as though she was assessing a classroom. Finished with her assessment, she quickly moved into action. Mrs. Sorenzen was fun to watch. She had a bolder voice and more energy than anyone could have anticipated coming out of someone who weighed no more than 120 pounds. She had three huge sacks hanging from her arms and started pulling items out by the handful. She had obviously picked up more than nail polish. She seemed to know all about hospital waiting areas and what people might want. She pulled out some updated magazines, a newspaper, some Marshmallow Rice Krispy treats, sodas, and some of her homemade cinnamon rolls. I didn't think I was hungry, but I had to admit, they smelled great.

She had also purchased many more bottles than anyone could have expected, but it certainly made Mrs. Hawkins smile. She told Joyce, "I just knew that I could count on you."

Mrs. Sorenzen spoke like a politician. "If it's important to a friend, then it's important to me, and if it's important to me, I'm going to go all the way. Besides, you know that I've always got you covered girl. Now, Sadie, just what are you going to do with this? I'm gonna' bet that you're plannin' to paint Harper's nails just to perk her up. At least I can't imagine that you're going to paint Max's nails. Am I right?"

Mrs. Hawkins let out an unchecked chuckle that seemed to blend in with her sniffles. In the midst of chuckling, she explained the nickname of Sadie, although most had heard it before or could readily figure it out. Obviously, Mrs. Sorenzen was an incredibly close friend. She was also the one who had given Lucie the nickname Sadie. After explaining the nickname to the younger ones in the group, Mrs. Hawkins told Joyce the details covering the comments regarding fingernails and outlined her plan. All of that seemed to delight Mrs. Sorenzen who announced, "Girl, you and I think alike. I think God is tellin' you something, and, if not, it's givin' us something to do besides sit around havin' a pity party. So, let's not just make those nails pretty, lets have them say something as well. How about 'hang on' or something like that, and paint the letters upside down so that Harper can read them when she gets better?" This last comment prompted some more tears from Lucie and another hug for Mrs. Sorenzen.

It was agreed, and the waiting room immediately turned into a nail salon. Mrs. Hawkins, Mrs. Sorenzen, Aunt Beth, Corina, and Mrs. Schuler all went to work and painted each other's nails. They also made each of the guys have at least one nail painted. None dare refuse, although Max kept shaking his head. The base of each nail would be pink and the letters or symbols would be purple or violet. On the guys' nails the letter "E" for Ellie was painted, but I was the exception. On both of my index fingers, Mrs. Hawkins painted the letter "H" for Harper. Although somewhat bewildered at this unique method of support, I reluctantly agreed. In the end, I proudly revealed my two painted nails to Corina.

In spite of this upbeat activity, my whole body was rigid and sick with tension, and I still felt like a cloud shadowed the room. I continued to feel confused and afraid and worried and overwhelmed. I could only sort out a few things and constantly found myself thinking, what is going on here, and how can the women act this way? I wanted to lie on the floor, curl up in a fetal position, and cry like a baby and, yet, here the ladies were focusing on fingernails. This didn't seem to me to be a rational way of helping anything. I had been assured that Harper would live, but I wanted her awake and talking.

Within an hour of Mrs. Sorenzen's arrival, each of us got to go into Harper's ICU room to visit for a short time. As my turn to visit came and as I entered, I found Mrs. Hawkins sitting on the edge of Harper's bed meticulously painting Harpo's nails. The upside down letters spelled "hanging on" and had a cross in between the two words.

Although seeing the nails was helpful, my worried gaze fixed on the antiseptic smear around the top of her chest, the tube in her throat, the light sheet over her chest, the wires hooked all over my Harper, and the noise of the machines all around. Harper looked so tiny and helpless and sick. Tears kept busting out of the corner of my eyes and dripped on the sheet as I leaned in to kiss her forehead. My knees wanted to buckle. I gently squeezed her wrist and rubbed her arm and whispered how special she was. Mrs. Hawkins smiled and told me, "We will get through this. You just keep hanging in there too."

I had gone in with Corina and Mrs. Schuler. I tried to focus on Harper's face, but my gaze kept going back to the ventilator or respirator. Whatever it was called, it was downright scary to see this contraption stuck in her mouth. It looked more like a giant insect sucking the life out of her instead of a helpful tool. No amount of verbal information fully prepares a person for the visual impact of seeing someone in that situation. I felt helpless.

Although Harper had occasionally opened her eyes, she hadn't responded to anyone except her mom and that was only a brief hand squeeze. The ICU nurse, Lydia, explained to others, who had visited before me, that the sedation from the surgery was still wearing off and assured all that "she wasn't in pain." I think she also said that Harper was receiving some other meds, but the details of exactly what she said were fuzzy. I thought to myself, I could sure use some medicine if people expect me to hang on, but I didn't say it out loud. At least, I don't think I said it out loud.

Following my visit to Harper's room and after an hour or so, Mrs. Hawkins came out to talk to all of us in the waiting room with an update.

Harper was awake and a different doctor dealing with the breathing tube, along with a breathing therapist, had come in to take Harper off the vent. These two specialists intended to monitor Harper for a few minutes to see how she handled breathing on her own. Mrs. Hawkins had preferred not to watch so she had stepped out.

Eventually, Lydia, the ICU nurse, came out and motioned Mrs. Hawkins back in. Max followed on her heels. In twenty to thirty minutes Mrs. Hawkins came back out with some new tears. Lydia and this other doctor seemed to think that Harper was having trouble swallowing, but was breathing well on her own. Dr. Alexander, the surgeon, and Dr. Mills had been notified and all seemed to be concerned that Harper may have had a small stroke. So far the effects had appeared to be limited and for now they were leaving her off the vent. Lydia also indicated that a neurologist might be coming in to do an assessment and that a scan of some kind might be ordered. I was losing count of the number of doctors and specialists dealing with Harper.

After Mr. and Mrs. Hawkins shared this latest concern, the whole group in near unison started asking questions. The common theme of the various questions followed; "What do they mean by mild stroke, what happened, and so, what's really wrong?"

The answer or response to each question eventually came from Max. He said, "Again, it looks like she's having some trouble swallowing. They haven't given her anything to drink, but somehow, they can tell by watching her. I'm really not sure. As she wakes up, we will know more, but they said that they want to check other things like her speech. Again, we were told to be patient and let her fully wake up. The good news, at least for now, is that she does not seem to have any paralysis of her limbs, her heart sounds great, and she's breathing well. Finally, they said we should know more before the day is over."

"God, when is this day going to be over," I thought? I was relieved by the earlier words of Dr. Mills, "Yes, she will live", and with Max's "good news", but I was left with too many other words like "if" and "later". I didn't want to wait for an absolute, certain, clear, positive answer. This whole process seemed to be more than I could possibly process mentally. I wanted to do something, to take action, to kill the bad guy, but I couldn't locate the enemy to fight it. I was back to sitting and waiting. If I had been in charge of designing a hell for me, it would be sitting in the status of the unknown, the not knowing, and the not being able to fix it. I felt like the "druggers" on the street, dying just a little bit at a time.

    I planned to stay at the hospital that whole night and all of the next day. I wanted to see Harper awake and I wanted to hear what the neurologist's evaluation would reveal. Before I fell asleep in a chair, I tried to think, but couldn't complete any thought. It may have been because I was so tired, but it was also because the image of fingernails kept flying into my thinking and messing up any logical pattern of thought. Before I fell asleep I wondered, "Is there a theory of fingernails?"

CHAPTER EIGHT
Knock Knock – Who's There

There is nothing as uncomfortable as sleeping in a chair at a hospital. I've had horrible nights before, but that had to have been one of the worst. The only good thing that came out of it was that each awakening would prompt me to check on Harper. Each time I went into the room, Mrs. Hawkins was in the recliner next to Harper's bed, and no matter how quietly I entered the room, she would open her eyes, smile at me, and give me a thumbs up.

It was almost unnerving to have someone act so positively in a time of crisis, but she certainly made me feel that I was not only welcome, but also a part of that family's inner circle. I had never had an inner circle involving adults before. Harper seemed to sleep on and off, but I wasn't sure how. The ICU nurse seemed to be in the room every few minutes. As the night wore on, Mrs. Hawkins continued to smile, but I wondered, why is it that some smiles in life look sad?

Although Tuesday wasn't perfect, the health news surrounding my girl had become more understandable, and I felt like I had a better picture of what to expect from that point on. There had been a parade of doctors and therapists through her room that morning and I had little chance to be one-on-one with her. However, by that afternoon, Harper recognized me, reached out her hand, and gave me a little smile. I wanted to hug her, but that wasn't allowed. As I looked at her, I could see how she was having some trouble with her mouth and throat and, although she appeared to mouth some words, she didn't speak out loud to me. The assessment process would continue, but the preliminary information suggested that Harper was having some speech problems in addition to the swallowing matter. Lydia, the ICU nurse, was back on duty that day and summarized some of what the professionals were saying and told us that Harper would probably require some rehabilitation services, including speech therapy. They also discovered when they tried to set her up, that she had limited balance. The bottom line seemed to be that when she got out of ICU in a couple of days, they would move her to acute care and then on to a regular cardiac bed. However, after that, she might end up in a rehab unit. It was interesting to see how on target Dr. Mills' assessment and predictions had been right after surgery.

    I caught a ride to my house that Tuesday evening. I needed to get back to school on Wednesday. When I entered my house, no one even asked where I had been or what was going on with Harper even though all three were home. Little Maria was watching TV as usual and barely looked up. Mom was sitting in a chair with either a heating pad or cold pack on her face. I assumed she must have had one of her headaches. JJ had just grabbed a beer out of the fridge and, although he gave me a dirty look, he seemed sullen and didn't stare me down like he sometimes did.

    That evening, I fixed a sandwich, got a bottle of water, and retreated to my cell as quickly as possible. I was intent on keeping a low profile. With everything else, I didn't need an eruption on the home front. I was juggling enough as it was and school needed immediate attention. I had great grades and a lofty standing at school and wanted to keep it. I wasn't sure I could make it for two more years, but if I could, I knew that college was probably my only way out of my maddening life. A term paper was due, I had an algebra test coming up, I had a project in Spanish to complete, and I was involved in forensics club activities. Once I got into the books or any project, I actually enjoyed them, but I was sometimes overwhelmed when I looked at them on my calendar. Instead of taking just one day at a time, my tendency was to lump them together, brood about them, and work myself into a panic. So, I had one of my talks with myself, like Mrs. Sheppard had told me to do, and settled in on the term paper. I had an old radio with some headphones and tried to shut out the last few days, tried to block out where I was, tried to set my worries about

Harper on the shelf, and refused to even think about my longer-term future so that I would only look at the project in front of me. I had to have that talk several times, but, in the end, I made great progress on my homework that evening.

All went extremely well at school on that Wednesday. I gave lots of information about Harper to her friends and Mrs. Sheppard. The update to Mr. Smith on my term paper went well, and I was quickly caught up in my other classes and on my projects. The only difficulty was my focus. My mind seemed to constantly wander off to Harper. I finally tucked my fingers into the palms of my hands so that I wouldn't look at my painted nails, because each time that I saw them, it would trigger a myriad of thoughts about Harpo.

That evening and each evening for the next ten days, I focused on visiting Harper at the Med Center. I had access to several rides and, if one fell through, I was an expert on the city bus. Manny was flexible with my work. Again, it seemed he was helping in the only way he could figure. Harper was moved to a regular bed in the cardiac unit, and Mr. and Mrs. Hawkins said that they expected her to be moved to a rehab unit of the hospital or a rehab center any day. Except for Harper's speech and balance issues, she had improved rapidly. A speech therapist came into her room daily. A respiratory therapist had also been coming in, but he was no longer needed. The multiple doctors and therapists indicated that Harper's heart and breathing and most other functions were doing great. In addition, her swallowing improved to the point that she was able to eat soft foods. Although her speech issues and balance problems were obvious, I was glad she was alive and awake. By now, many people had assured me over and over that Harper's life was no longer at risk, but it was difficult for me to trust, so I still worried. Gradually, I felt more secure about her life and felt that I could live with any complication.

Unlike me, though, Harper was not feeling relieved. Harper was depressed and often deep in the dumps. She was accustomed to speaking clearly and using the exact words she wanted. Even after ten days, she was constantly struggling with words and having difficulty expressing herself. At times, she would be so mad and frustrated that she would pick something up off her tray and throw it. When she mixed up important words or couldn't pronounce a word, she would break down and cry. Of course, she would mainly cry when she wasn't otherwise busy throwing something. Sometimes, though, she would do both at the same time. This was not the Harper I knew. I knew that my Happy Harper was in there somewhere, but on the outside, it seemed that she had become a different person.

On April fourth, the tenth day after the surgery, she tried to explain to me how frustrated she had been trying to walk that morning. Even with assistance, she said that she kept "bumbling" around. I knew that probably her intended word was "stumbling", but the error made her frustrated, and she made a growling sound in anger. Immediately after that word mix up, she tried to tell me to come over to the chair she was sitting in. She evidently wanted to show me something, but I didn't know what she meant when she said, "comb over hair" instead of "come over here." Before I could even process anything, she slammed her hand down on a tray nearby and tears were coming out of her eyes.

Her frustration hadn't become a full-blown tantrum yet, but when in jest I said, "You think I'd look better if I did a comb over of my hair?" She picked up an empty plastic cup and winged it my way. Fortunately, I caught the cup and made a wise choice to quickly go to her chair and calm her. I said, "Look, I was teasing and maybe I shouldn't have been. I know how frustrated you are, but I just couldn't pass that up. In fact, I think that you should talk more to me instead of giving up and talking less. Let's make it a game and enjoy it. We've got to do something besides getting mad every time a word gets mixed up. You know how we used to have fun making up Knock, Knock jokes?" She shook her head up and down, but she wasn't quite ready to let me off the hook. She still had a fist flexed and tears in her eyes. Regardless, I stayed with my angle. "Girl, I know you just mixed up those words unintentionally, but if we used them right, they could be another Knock, Knock joke. Now let's try it. I'll say, knock, knock, and you will answer. Now, knock, knock."

She let out a sigh, unclenched her right fist, and with effort got out, "Who's there?" She even smiled a bit after the words came out.

I said, "Comb over hair."

She appropriately but very slowly replied, "Comb over hair who?" Her smile got bigger, and she ended with a tiny giggle.

I then said, "Comb over hair right now and give me a kiss." By that time, I had moved to her side, leaned closely towards her, and touched her cheek. She touched my face in return, kissed me on the forehead, and followed with a giggle. The process seemed to relax her, so I told her that we would work on some more jokes, slow things down, and just do the best we could each day.

After Harper and I discussed our plan some more, Harper's dad came into the room, and the idea was shared. He seemed quite pleased, especially after Harper gave him the two thumbs up. In fact, after he thought about it for a moment, he came over, patted me on the back, and said, "I think this is a great idea, and it's something that all of us can do, ah, except me. You know, I don't play games." He followed this with a shrug of his shoulders, his head slightly tilted, raised eyebrows, and a smile that indicated, "that's the way it is and you know it".

From that point on, even as Harper was moved into rehab the next day, we worked on jokes. We even pulled the therapists into the routine. They said it "played right into their plans." They explained that one of the daily activities was to play games, including word games.

Over the next week, we made up some good jokes, but most were horribly bad. Even with the bad ones though, Harper seemed to have a good time. If one of our jokes was really bad, she would pretend to choke as though she was having trouble swallowing again, and she would follow it with a comment that became her trademark reaction. She would try to mimic one of boxer Muhammad Ali's old lines by saying something like, "I'm still the greatest and you ain't. You just used a choke-a-joke insteada' a rope-a-dope. You need to get outta da ring before you get hurt." She eventually got to the point where she could say it clearly.

Our favorite joke was the one Harper came up with about an unsuccessful one-armed hunter. It seemed the hunter couldn't hit any birds. Her punch line was, "You know what they always say; no arm, no fowl." She would follow her jokes, even the ones that weren't funny, and her "rope-a-dope" comments with bouts of laughter. Her laughter would trigger ours. Mr. and Mrs. Hawkins were delighted and appreciative of the progress and often thanked me. Hearing Harpo laugh and seeing her have some happy times were all the thanks I needed.

Almost a week later, Harper's balance had improved enough that she was able to go home. She wasn't pleased that she still had to rely on a walker, but she was ecstatic about going home. The treatment and recovery process had been difficult, but it had also been amazingly positive and productive. Harper's outlook was no less than unlimited. Harper's dad said that she was back to her old self. Although in some ways that was true, in other ways the experiences in the hospital would change us all forever. As we exited the hospital it felt like we were different people than when we had entered.

The day Harper was to head home was a Friday. That Friday fell exactly four weeks after that first appointment with Dr. Guss. Dr. Guss had evidently called my mom several times and talked to her by phone. It seemed that he had been insistent on her coming into his office for an interview. After numerous attempts and much urging, she had agreed and was told to bring me on that Friday. On that day, I had a "believe-it-or-not" moment when she actually parked the car with me in it and walked into the shrink's office with me. All the way through the hospital corridors, I expected her to turn around and bolt. I even made a bet with myself that she run before getting to the office. I was wrong.

We walked into the old building housing the psych unit, punched the fourth floor button on the antiquated elevator, and entered Dr. Guss' office. We arrived only five minutes late. As we entered, Maggie asked my mom how bad her bout with the flu had been. My mom said, "I ain't had it this year and I'm hopin' I don't get it."

Upon hearing my mom's comment, Maggie shot me a playful but accusing expression. I could practically hear her say, "You rat!"

Even though it was a few minutes past the time for the appointment, Dr. Guss yelled out of his open, office door, "I'll be right there, just have a seat." It looked like he was reviewing my green file and making some notes. I sat down, but Mom stood looking around. She searched her purse for her cigarettes. After finding them, she put them right back as she remembered she couldn't smoke in the hospital. She started pacing, coughed, and paced some more. I watched her as she glanced towards the exit. I continued to silently make a bet that she was going to take off. She acted like a little kid debating the merits of stepping into a haunted house on Halloween. Finally, Dr. Guss came out and said, "Well, Mrs. Martinez, it's nice to finally meet you in person."

She responded with, "I don't go by Martinez any more, you can call me Maria or Mrs. Johnson. Even though I ain't changed my name formal or nothing, that's what I want to be called."

Dr. Guss quickly came back with, "OK. That works for me. Mrs. Johnson, I'd like to go over some things with you first. We can bring Buck in right after that." He put his hand out for Mom to go in before him, he followed, and he closed the door behind them. I wondered which chair she picked.

Maggie was still looking at me with that look, but she also had a bit of a smirk. I smiled back and said, "You caught me. What was I supposed to do? I was just trying to cover for her. I didn't mean to make you nervous about, you know, the flu thing. I'm sorry." If I had shut up and ended with those comments, I would have been fine, but I said the next sentence, and it came out awkwardly. "Are you feeling as good as you look?"

She laughed and didn't seem offended. "I'm really feeling great. Thanks for asking. I just hope you're not feeding me another line of bull like you did the last time you were here. By the way, I think I now understand. In fact the more I think about it, if I have a boy, I hope he grows up to be as clever as you."

As my conversation with Maggie continued, I was beginning to relax. Our pleasant banter was soon interrupted, however, at about the fifteen minute mark. As I listened, I could tell there had been a temperature change inside Dr. Guss' private office. Things had gotten heated. I heard no complete interchanges and I could only understand some of Dr. Guss' words, so I really didn't know what caused the change, but the volume of the voices definitely went up a notch. I could hear my mom's raspy voice, but not individual words. Although I couldn't hear a completed thought from Dr. Guss, I could hear snippets of his part of the conversation. I heard "Why not JJ," and "Yes, he is special," and "I can't do it any other way," and after I heard the words, "Well, you make the decision," the door opened. Mom charged out of his office, marched through the reception area, and hightailed it down the hallway before I could even move. Even though I had earlier thought she would run, I was surprised with this delayed reaction and was left sitting with my mouth open. I thought I'd have won the bet with myself if she had run sooner.

As Dr. Guss came out, he looked disgusted and disappointed, but his look was certainly not aimed at me. He glanced towards the hallway first and then looked to me. He found me smiling. Then he chuckled. I wasn't sure why I was smiling except maybe I was thinking, "See what I mean." Either way, without saying a word, we seemed to have a mutual moment of appreciation.

Dr. Guss sat down on the arm of a chair in the empty reception room. Dr. Guss and Maggie exchanged glances and Maggie tactfully got up and went into what looked like a workroom or copy room and closed the door behind her. Once alone, Dr. Guss looked me in the eye, let out a sigh and said, "Well" in an elongated expression of the word that made it seem like it took five seconds to say. He paused, fidgeted, looked at the floor as if thinking for a moment, and then fixed back on my eyes. He acted like he was going to talk to me right there, but after what looked like an internal debate, he invited me into his office and closed the door to share where things stood.

After another pause and after a couple of bouts of rubbing his face with his left hand, Dr. Guss finally spoke. From that point on, he proceeded to cover things pretty quickly. He began with another "well", but got right to the point. "Well, I guess this is where we stand." In summary, he said that he could no longer keep setting appointments because my mom was unwilling to participate and unwilling to talk about anything except what she deemed to be my problems. She had also not consented for me to see him on my own anymore. He told me to call him anytime if I considered myself to be in danger or to ask him for a resource phone number. He gave me an additional phone number to reach him even after hours. I thought to myself that he's a lot like Mrs. Sheppard.

He told me another thing that explained some about my first appointment. He confirmed that my mom had first called at the urging of the social worker from protective services. The social worker had indeed told my mom that the family could use some family counseling. Dr. Guss would be required to tell the social worker that my mom was no longer in contact with him. Dr. Guss planned to live up to his word and limit his comments, but he didn't know what action his call might set off with social services or how my mom might react to the call. He was concerned and asked me what I thought. I said very little in response but did say that I would continue as I had for the past few weeks and try to keep a low profile.

As I shared some about how I'd kept a low profile the past few weeks, I gave him the short version of Harper's story. He was fascinated. He listened and interacted as though he actually knew her and cared about her. He ended with "Buck, I really wish I had known all of this." He paused, looked at me with a sad look, and then asked, "Now, how are you getting home?"

"Remember, Big Red and I've done this before. If I'm over this way again, though, I'll talk you into buying me a meal."

As I went out the door, his final words were, "Buck, you truly are a special young man. I hope I see you again. By the way, don't forget, if you feel you are in danger, there really are people who care and who you can call."

I wished I could count on that. I knew he meant well, but I had learned from the past that by the time I recognized danger it had been too late to intercept it. I picked up my heavy survival pack that also served as my book bag, swung it in a semi-circle, and worked to balance the weight of survival on my back. With it secured, I turned down the hallway by myself. Unfortunately, I had to consider Dr. Guss to be in my rear-view mirror and gone with the first step out the door.

It was a joke to think that Mom would ever participate in counseling. I thought to myself, knock, knock, who's there? Not Mom.

CHAPTER NINE
Salvaged Musings

Instead of hanging around the hospital and hustling a free meal, I decided to head back towards my neighborhood, so that I could visit Milo. I had been making the trek down Sage Drive more frequently lately. Visiting with Milo was like using Google without a computer. Generally, he could pull information out of his head on nearly any subject. His passion for reading and contemplating life, in general, gave him a wealth of insight. He especially understood human behavior, but most importantly, he listened. After each visit to this unlikely oasis, I felt better. He gave advice, if asked, but mostly he would listen, let the story unfold, and only then give his thoughts that might allow me to sort things out. When it came to life problems, he didn't like to think of himself as giving answers as much as giving new ways to see things and telling stories about some of his hard-earned lessons.

Milo had this tendency to let me share about an event or subject until the water turned "completely muddy", as he put it. His own humorous description of what he did was, "Well, Buck, I wait until just the right moment, and then I drop my word bomb like a kid doing a cannonball into a dirty pool." His bombs would send ripples through my head and usually cut to the heart of the matter being discussed. Milo's cannonballs were usually not lengthy. He had this knack for using words efficiently and reducing certain complex issues down to manageable points. Unfortunately, some remained complex.

Milo's offerings always came with disclaimers. He would preface with, "You realize that I had to learn this the hard way. I seem to only learn through my mistakes." He would often add an example from his life. One of his insights that he applied more than once was, "Bad isn't good and most bad has no good reason, but sometimes out of bad can come good." He used this several times during my visits in March and April.

Each time he said that phrase, I would counter with, "Well, I'm still waiting on the good." He would remain serious and tell me to keep looking. I would then explain that he was contradicting Manny's advice to not look under rocks. Milo would laugh, but he would also relate how much his life was changing and improving. He made it clear that he was now reaping some of that "good". Looking around at his living arrangements, I could only wonder about that. Occasionally, when speaking about the good, Milo would allude to something about faith in his life, but he never went into detail. He would always say something about, "you aren't quite ready for that discussion." I didn't know what he meant, but I really didn't want to go there either.

When I arrived that afternoon, Milo was not at the camp's entry point by the gnarly old fence. It was not necessary for him to be at his post until later. That wasn't an issue, however, as I didn't need an escort and no one in camp would be surprised to see me. This had become familiar ground. In fact, I knew each step of the way down the five-foot wide, winding trail that led to the camp. The first tent was only about fifty yards from the wooden gateposts if a direct route could have been taken. The distance, however, was a bit more than that on the trail, and the trail was really the only available access around the weeds and thorny vines. I found comfort and even enjoyment in the short walk and always felt like I was entering friendly territory.

It wasn't difficult to spot Milo's tent. His was the largest tent, and it had some real thinking behind it. I loved his ingenuity and the manner in which he used discarded material in such clever ways. I called his structure the "double-wide". Milo was not only a "scrounger", as he called it, but he was a selective and inventive scrounger. On the day before and the day of trash pick up, he would walk a circuit of the neighborhood and pick out items that he could put to use. He saw things in salvage that few people would recognize. He also had an arrangement with a remodeling crew to give him some items before they paid to take them to a landfill. Some of the items were still in excellent condition. With those items, Milo assumed that the property owners had just wanted a change.

He used wooden pallets on the floor and covered them with nice looking carpet remnants from the contractor's trash. He had two layers of blue tarp covering the tent's top and sides. The outside layer, a heavy-duty tarp, was without openings, while the inside layer, a lighter weight tarp, had window-like openings. Each of those openings was covered with screen wire that was duct-taped in place. The window openings on the inside layer were intended to allow air into the tent on warm days or as needed. On those days, Milo would pull up the outside tarp to reveal the window openings.

For walls and insulation, he used extra long, large screen, television boxes stuffed with Styrofoam. These were also taped together. He had two beds. The mattresses sat on top of wooden crates. The single person mattresses had been donated from Catholic Charities. He had four chairs, a battery operated light, and a charcoal grill outside. For winter months, he even created his own solar heating system. His solar method involved using as many as fifty, two-liter, plastic bottles. He partially filled each bottle with water, painted each of them black on one side of the bottle, and tied them to the tarp around the base of the tent as both ballast to hold down the tarp and as elements to capture heat. In the summer, he just turned the bottle over with the black side down.

These were just the items readily visible. Milo had other items and useful tools stored in the various wooden boxes. I asked him how he had come up with the ideas. He said that he had once seen a picture showing Teddy Roosevelt in one of his big-game, hunting tents and that "my tent had to be better than Teddy's." He followed this comment with loud laughter. Milo could be thoughtful and very serious, but he could also laugh and have fun. I appreciated both sides of him. Milo was a rarity in the homeless camp, but that rarity made him special and was one of the many reasons he was referred to as Mayor Milo and even Judge Milo when it came to dispute resolution within the camp.

As I entered the main camp area, I encountered other men standing outside their tent. Their shelters looked like they could blow over in the slightest wind. The insides were the pits. Their ramshackle collections were in disarray. The mattresses looked matted, and the men, standing next to their hovels, were dirty. Again, unlike Milo's area, their areas had the smell of waste. Regardless, I waved and said "hello" to each man. People living in the camp spent as much time outside their tents as the weather allowed. Outside represented the kitchen and living room for most. Most cooked on grills that had been retrieved and recycled from trash. Others used grates covering campfires. Outside was also the place for visiting. As often as possible, the tents were seen as the bedrooms and used for sleeping or for retreating during the cold and rain. Unfortunately, the tents were also retreats from occasional arguments that would erupt, especially when one or more had been drinking too much. I knew all about that kind of retreat.

As I sauntered in, the camp dog, a mixed mutt that Milo said was at least partially a terrier, ran up to me barking a raspy little bark. Milo called him Rat, but the rest of the camp called him Rip. For a while, I thought I was simply misunderstanding, but when I asked Milo about it on prior visits, he said, "No, we call him different things. I don't like Rip. Besides he's here to chase the rats off, so I call him Rat." Milo never explained why he didn't like the name Rip.

I saw Milo cooking on his grill. He smiled a big smile, waved me over and said, "You're just in time for Spam night." He had explained before what Spam was, but I liked it anyway. He had also explained that any night could potentially be "Spam night".

"What are you up to this fine Friday evening, Buck?"

"Oh, I just came from an appointment at the Med Center and thought you might have a chance to visit."

"You bet. Let me add on another couple of slices, give them a little heat and char, and I'll be ready. Go on in, grab a water or soda, and make yourself at home."

I went into his tent, picked out a water bottle from his cooler and a folding chair. I noticed he had some books and papers lying on a different chair. The open page of the worn pamphlet had something about a "higher power" at the top of the page. I put my chair near his and near the grill and relaxed while he finished grilling and heating veggies in an open can. I adjusted both chairs to face west. If we talked into the evening, I wanted to watch the sunset. From my room at my house, I could never see the sunrise or sunset.

When done, Milo sat down and wasted no time in opening the conversation. He issued the friendly directive, "Well, let's hear it."

I recapped the events covering the last couple of days with Mom and JJ. Milo cut through all of that with, "So, nothing has changed on that front."

I followed with a complete account of my trip to the Med Center, what I had overheard between Dr. Guss and Mom, and the outcome. The outcome covered both my mom's departure and Dr. Guss' parting message. By the time I ended the description of events, Milo had finished his two spam sandwiches and his drink and was wiping his mouth. He took two or three minutes before speaking. It was common for him to delay his response. I realized that he was giving me a chance to add anything I wanted to add, and I also realized that he was letting it all sink in. I picked up my food and started to eat.

When he finished thinking and when he realized that I had finished my recollection of events, he offered his usual disclaimer and caution. "You do realize that you will need to listen to this twice before you begin to get it. Don't you?"

He started in a slow, deliberate tempo. "People are often more committed to their problems than they are committed to allowing feedback or looking for solutions. They are more committed to the problem, because they view their specific behavior in a totally different light than others around them do. In fact, from their perspective, they often see that same behavior as a solution and not the problem at all. They see it as a solution to another, totally different set of issues in their life. They are blind to an alternate view. In my opinion there is very little hope for change until and only if that perspective changes. Yes, sometimes their position involves illogical denial, but they will hang on until the bitter end, and often the end is bitter and even tragic."

He had just cannonballed a word bomb into my muddy water and the ripples had become waves splashing around my ears. I had learned to sit back and let all of the words soak in before doing anything else. Milo repeated his message. He said the exact same thing a second time and said it more slowly. I was able to understand a bit more, but I was having a tough time connecting any of this to Mom and JJ.

Milo then added an example from his life that was related to his drinking. Milo explained that he had once justified his excessive drinking, his drinking while at work, his excessive spending on alcohol, and his partying as various forms of his solution to escape his rocky marriage and to relieve the stresses from his law practice. A few friends around him said he had a drinking problem, but he gradually stopped hanging around them. He instead started relying more and more on people who made excuses for him.

"I denied my sick addiction right up until my marriage failed, until my law practice suffered, and until my emergency room visit."

He explained that these failures became the wake up calls he needed before he could change perspective. Only then, and only out of desperation, did he really come to grips with the same problem that others had seen. Even then, he needed intervention, AA, and the Twelve-Step Program to give him new hope and to give him support in dealing with his addiction. He pointed to others in the camp and said that some may never change and that an early death or imprisonment will be the end result. For some, he predicted that outcome to be very near.

Milo continued with, "I ran away from any effort to confront me about my drinking out of fear and denial. I couldn't live with how it was affecting my law practice, but I also didn't want to accept that I was an alcoholic and needed help. This information doesn't help you to solve the situation you find yourself in, but it may help you to understand that you aren't the problem. Your mom is making you the scapegoat. If she didn't, she would more than likely be obligated to face something in her own life that she is just too afraid to confront. Some people are never able to get the real issues on the table and they pay a heavy price. She's setting herself up for that kind of hard knock."

He repeated his original starting point a third time. For me, some of the mud was starting to settle. "Milo, thank you. You're right, it doesn't solve anything, but it sure makes me feel better about myself." We sat around for another thirty minutes and watched the sky. He grabbed two snack cakes out of a box and we devoured them.

After the interlude, I took one more shot at talking about Mom and JJ. I told Milo that I thought that I understood, at least partially, what he said about how Mom and I were probably looking at the same events from different perspectives, but I still wondered why she and JJ always seemed so angry with me. I asked, "Why does Mom let JJ beat on me? She knows what's going on."

Milo again took his time and, as he started to speak, I braced for another splash. "You know, Buck, anger and hurt can look alike, and they often originate from the same source or incident in one's life. The only difference is usually how the feelings and emotions are acted out. Some take it out on other people, while some take it out on themselves. Actually, it's not uncommon for individuals to take it out on both self and others at the same time. Now, I don't know where JJ's hurt comes from, but he is certainly taking it out on you, and back to my other comment, for some reason, your mom sees JJ as some kind of solution to something in her life. She must have a deep hurt, loneliness, sickness, or void in her life to choose JJ over you. We may never know the source. Who knows, it could just be the fact that you're named after your dad and you're catching all the hell that's aimed at him."

Milo's second attempt was much more revealing and I understood more. Even with the understanding, I told Milo, "Well, understanding it doesn't make it hurt any less, and I can't and won't take much more."

Milo listened and only said, "Let me know when you need me because I can do more than listen."

Even though I didn't know what more he could do, I still needed to hear someone say that to me. I tucked his offer away in the survival compartment of my brain. That compartment was expanding.

We stopped talking about JJ and Mom. Discussing them always seemed heavy. We needed to balance the night out by talking about something we enjoyed.

Of course, my joy was Harper, so my conversation came around to her and our jokes. I got Milo to laughing, especially about our Knock, Knock jokes. Milo and I agreed that a good sense of humor was one of the best things any of us could possess in life. Milo also understood how frustrating it could be when not understood or how frustrating it can be to not understand. This triggered in Milo a story about one of his old cases.

THE SECRETS OF CUTTING GRASS

Milo told of an accident case he had handled early in his career. Milo was defending one of the drivers and the police report listed a witness to the accident, a Mr. B. K. Hobbs. Milo couldn't contact Mr. Hobbs prior to the hearing, so he sent out a subpoena and, sure enough, Mr. Hobbs appeared at the last minute. In any event, Milo had called Mr. Hobbs to the witness stand and started to question him. Milo told the story like he was reading two parts in a play. He would identify who was speaking by saying their name first.

Bailiff: Do you swear to tell the truth, the whole truth and nothing but the truth so help you God?

Hobbs: "Well, I knowed what I seen. I'll tell that truth."

Judge: "It's I do or I will."

Hobbs: "Well, how can you tell it?"

Judge: "No, not my answer, yours."

Hobbs: "Oh, OK. I'm gonna do true."

Milo: "Would you state your name and address and tell the court where you were on the day in question?"

Hobbs: "Well, I was bornt in the State of Missouri, but I don't recount the address. I wasn't old enough to knowed that yet."

Milo: "Ok, let's skip that and get right to the accident. I understand from the police report that you witnessed the accident, recognized one of the drivers, and stopped to help. Is that right."

Hobbs: "No."

Milo: "No, what?"

Hobbs: "What?"

Milo: "Would you explain what you saw?"

Hobbs: "I seed my friend Eddie get out of the car. He was holding his arm. It was broke clear through. He was yelling."

Milo: "So, you knew the one driving the car at that time?"

Hobbs: "No."

Milo: "I thought you said you knew Eddie?"

Hobbs: "Yes, but he weren't driverin' the car right then. He was out in the street yellin'."

Milo stopped telling the long version of the story at that point and summarized that it had taken nearly forty minutes to establish that Hobbs had absolutely no information relevant to the actual cause of the wreck. After Hobbs was excused, the Judge took a break, and called Milo into his office. The Judge laughed and said that it had been as good as listening to the famous Abbott and Costello routine of "Who's On First." Still, the Judge had chewed Milo out for calling a witness without interviewing him first.

Milo reflected that, at the time, "I was never so embarrassed in my life."

After that incident with Hobbs and for the next year, when Milo was in court in front of that Judge, the Judge would always smile and ask Milo if he had interviewed all the witnesses. Other attorneys had heard about the famous B. K. Hobbs and would ask Milo if he was going to find Hobbs and call him that day, just to delay the case or just to add some humor.

As Milo reflected, he shared that the "Hobbs' event", as he called it, turned out to be one of the best things that ever happened to him as a young lawyer. Because of that case and that witness, Milo got to know a lot more people, especially as the story made its rounds. More importantly, as he had handled the teasing so well, judges and other attorneys thought well of Milo and liked him personally. It ended up being great for his reputation and for his business.

"So, Buck. You can tell Harper that she's not the only one in life who has struggled with finding the right words and with understanding. Tell her that's the truth, but also tell her how the story ended. In the final analysis, that incident had been good for me in several ways. Remember, bad isn't good and most bad has no good reason, but sometimes out of bad can come good."

I thought to myself, Milo can't even tell a joke without trying to teach something. I guess he was just using humor, much like I'd done with Harper. I wondered if Milo had become my rehab specialist.

"So, Milo, tell me again why you are living here. I bet there are other guys who have had drinking issues who aren't homeless. With your kind of talents, you don't have to be here, do you?"

Milo laughed. "Oh, you mean, why do I live here besides being absolutely penniless?" He paused, looked at his feet, and in a serious tone went on. "Poverty is certainly one of the reasons, but I guess it's also as much out of shame and out of a sort of self-exile from that other world. You're right. I know others who are what they call functional alcoholics. For me, though, I never want to be just functional. I don't want to pretend I'm doing my profession well when I know inside that I'm just getting by, or worse, that I know I'm screwing up. I tried that life for a few months last year, but I just couldn't stand myself."

"Well, I think I understand. For sure I get that you're one heck of a guy. I doubt there are many people who look at the world or look at themselves the way you do."

"You know, Buck, some people come here to live out of desperation and some to run-away. For me, it is an admission. It's my way to admit that I've hit bottom before I end up in jail, or dead, or God forbid, end up killing someone while I'm driving drunk."

I didn't need to ask any more, and he didn't need to say anymore. "Thanks, Milo."

We finished our drinks and watched the sky until the light faded. I got up to leave, told him "Catch you later", and walked back up the trail to the street. I needed to get some shut-eye as I was scheduled for two jobs the next day.

CHAPTER TEN
Postmortem Examinations

Saturday was going to be a busy day. I was scheduled to work at Manny's for my usual two hours. Then, I planned to catch the bus going north and get off near Hawkins Funeral Services. It was located between Corina and Harper's homes. Max had asked me to come in for two hours to help him clean up and to help him unpack large cases of cremation urns and stack the smaller boxes of urns on a shelf. He would pay me ten dollars an hour. I wanted the money and I thought it would be interesting to work and talk with Max, but the whole idea of working at the funeral home felt slightly creepy.

I finished at Manny's with five minutes to spare. I had put the last of the trash in the outside dumpster and was getting ready to check out. Before I could check out, Manny asked me to run out and put some cat litter on an oil spot near a gas pump and help him out at the counter for a few minutes. It was typical Manny. I knew his quick jobs and his few minutes could easily turn into twenty or thirty minutes. I told him about my other job, and that I could do one or the other, but not both. He asked me to put the absorbent on the oil spot. When I left, I had only put in an extra ten minutes. Not bad for working under Manny.

At the funeral home, I saw a long line of cars driving out of the funeral home parking lot. The slow moving procession followed the hearse and the large black funeral cars holding family members. I stopped walking about a half block away and stood watching the line of vehicles snake out and head west. I stood for at least ten minutes and, all the while, wondered. I wondered who had died, wondered how old they were, and wondered about the meaning of that person's life. Of course, my wondering went further and got weird. I wondered if all of these people were really going to miss the dead person or whether some of them were glad to see them gone. Thoughts about after-life tried to slip into my thinking, but, as usual, I kicked those thoughts out. I could only think up to the hole in the ground and hoped that it hadn't been a kid who died.

As the last car left with lights on and flashers blinking, I headed towards the building. I thought to myself that part of the job of cleaning up probably meant picking up after all those people.

When I got inside, a lady, wearing a nametag with Peggy S. on it, greeted me with, "Welcome to Hawkins. Which family are you with?"

I hesitated at the question and stumbled through my response.

"Hello, I'm Buck, and I'm not with any family. Max, I mean, Mr. Hawkins, told me to report in after lunch. He had some jobs that he wanted me to do here."

"Oh my. Yes. He did tell me that you were coming. I just forgot. You're that nice young man that Max keeps talking about. He just thinks the world of you. He's told me several times how you stuck by Harper after her surgery. He said you reminded him of the second dog in the book *Where The Red Fern Grows*. Oh, well, I don't mean that he called you a dog. Oh my, now how do I get out of that? Anyway, he didn't tell me how good looking you are. My. My. Now I can see another reason why Harper's so smitten with you."

As she talked, I felt like I was blushing. I didn't know if it was because of her comments on my "looks" or because her hand kept touching my arm. Her touch reminded me of Harper. Maybe that's why I was blushing. The "dog" comment didn't bother me at all and certainly wasn't the cause. I had read the book she mentioned, and I considered it a great read. I think I was like the loyal dog when it came to Harper. As I was thinking through all of that, I realized that she had my arm again, and that she was steering me out of the entryway and into a large room that held at least a hundred chairs.

As she moved into the large room, Peggy S. continued to talk at a fast clip. "I know that Max wanted you to start on this room. The service for Mrs. Daugherty just finished, and Max wanted this room cleaned as soon as possible. Our regular man is off today, and we need to move Mr. Metz in later today. So, the way to attack this is to take all of the chairs and move them to one side, get the vacuum from this closet right over here, and sweep the floor on the empty side. Then, move the chairs again and sweep the other side. Now, if you find trash on the floor, pick that up too. When you are done with that, I'll show you how to do the set-up for the next service and where to put all of the trash. Mr. Metz won't need all of this room, so we will set the chairs up in a different fashion. Also, when you are done, I'm sure Max will have you help bring the casket in and get the flowers set up. Did you get all of that?"

I hadn't said a word and yet her speech made me feel the need to take a breath. So, I smiled at her and took an exaggerated breath and breathlessly blurted out, "Yes Ma'am. I got all of that, but I do have a question."

It was obvious that she understood the tease and laughed. "People tell me all the time to slow down, but that's just the way I talk. What is your question?"

"Well, I really have two. First, what's your last name? I'd like to use it as we speak. My other question is whether you can generally tell me how the next set-up will look? If I know that, I can move the chairs back in such a way that the set-up might be easier. Would that be OK?"

"I think that's a great idea. Max told me that you were smart and polite. My, was he right. My last name is Snyder, but it's fine to call me Peggy, and I've got a paper that will actually show you the room layout for the next set-up. I'll get it while you're working. My, you are sharp. You must have good parenting," and she was off to the other room.

As she exited, I said, "Thank you, Mrs. Snyder." I selectively ignored her last comment about parenting and got to work. During the clean up, I found a few copies of the bulletins from the prior service and stopped working long enough to read Mrs. Daugherty's obituary. It was interesting to know her age and to see her list of family, but I wanted to know more. I wondered about what had been important to her, how people felt about her, and what people really knew about her. Maybe it was just this one obituary, but it seemed that a piece of paper revealed very little. Then I wondered. When I die, what would people say about me? Would my obituary say that I was a good student or would it say my mom thought I was mental? Then I wondered what would I want it to say?

An hour later, as Mr. Hawkins returned, I was done with the room and was in the middle of taking the trash out.

Mr. Hawkins came into the room, looked around, and exclaimed, "Wow, I didn't expect this to be done so quickly. This is great. Thank you. Buck, you've earned your pay already."

"Oh, you can thank Mrs. Snyder. She showed me what to do and where to find things. I understand that you might need some help rolling the casket in and setting up the flowers. Do you want to do that now or do you have something else for me to do?"

"That's exactly what we need to do. Follow me."

I followed him to a freight elevator that took us down one floor to a huge basement. Although this elevator was much larger, it sounded much like the one in the psych area of the hospital. It was also just as slow.

The basement had a gray, concrete floor that was spotless. Even though the area was neat and hospital-clean, it had a weird odor. It wasn't horrible, but neither was it pleasant.

In one corner of the basement near an outside double door, I noticed four cardboard cases that I guessed held the urns that I would soon unpack. As I looked in the opposite direction, I noticed four caskets still in crates. One of the crates had a piece of equipment under it. It looked like it was there to lift and move the crates. I knew people referred to that as a "dolly", but I didn't know why. As I looked around, I saw three other caskets with closed lids. Each had paperwork on the lid and looked occupied. A room off to the side had two stainless steel tables bolted to the floor. Each table had a large faucet-like fixture and sink attached to it and a large light overhead. In another area of the basement, I noticed two tables with large wheels that looked like hospital gurneys. Having gurneys made sense to me. Both hospitals and funeral homes wheel bodies around. It's just that some are dead and some alive.

I followed Mr. Hawkins around behind the elevator and saw a garage door. He pushed the automatic door opener revealing a hearse. Max opened the rear of the hearse and pulled out a fold-up gurney that looked similar to the ones used by ambulances. As he pulled it out, it unfolded and he rolled it over to me and told me to roll it over to the light colored, wooden casket at the other end of the basement. He closed up the hearse and garage door and followed me over. Once he had the wheels locked, he showed me how to help him slide the casket off a shelf and onto the gurney. Once on and secured, we rolled it to the elevator and into the room I had just cleaned.

"I always use the forklift to get the caskets up to a certain level and try to move them as little as possible. A casket weighs too much to move around very often. You might say they are dead weight." Mr. Hawkins chuckled at his own joke, and then explained, "Unfortunately, people in my business have a number of sick jokes."

In my serious mode and while taking everything in, I had missed the punch lines, but I finally got it and laughed. I told Max, "Harper and I needed you to help us out with our rehab jokes."

As we delivered the casket, Max complimented me on how well I followed directions, but also commented that I hadn't said much of anything during this whole process. "So, what are you thinking about, Buck?"

"Well, Sir, I was mainly just trying to listen and do what you needed, but I guess I was wondering about some things, that is, if you don't mind me asking."

"No problem, Buck. Ask anything you want."

"Well, doesn't dealing with death all the time kind of depress you and freak you out? I mean what do you think about at night after looking at dead bodies all day and seeing people all sad and crying? Doesn't it bother you to look at people all cold and naked? Don't you go home at night thinking about these people and worrying about dying yourself? I just wonder how you do this every day." I paused at this point and started to make fun of myself. "You probably figured out by now that I wonder about lots of things that most people don't even think about. You know, I'm kinda' weird that way."

Mr. Hawkins smiled and shook his head in much the same way that Dr. Guss had looked at me. "Buck, I think your questions are awesome. Really, questions like that reveal that you are a deep thinker. I've had some people ask me one of these questions before, but I've never had anyone throw them out at me all at once. I see your questions as your way of looking at life and wanting to know what it's all about. I love that attitude. In fact, I think looking for answers is the only way to find them."

Mr. Hawkins' encouragement was much like what I had received from Dr. Guss and Milo. I was starting to believe that I was, in fact, an okay guy. If only one person had told me that I was "all right", then I would still doubt. Yet, in the past few weeks, I had three adults, whom I respected, tell me the same thing. All I could do was tell Max, "Thanks."

"Well, I'm just saying what's true. Now Buck, I don't know if I'll get all of your questions covered in my answers today, but, maybe over time, I can get to most of them. To start with, I don't view my job as being all about death. I really get to know a lot about a person's life, especially when I visit with family members. Most of the families we deal with have been given lots of love by the person who died. When the living, loved ones share their memories, it makes me realize how valuable and meaningful certain lives were and are. Unfortunately, I also get to find out about lives that have been wasted and lives that have been focused on the destructive side of life. For those services, we usually see very few people in attendance. Often, there is not even a full service, just a reception that we call a visitation.

"Just last month, our county coroner mentioned something very similar to what I just said. The coroner came in with a body on which he had performed an autopsy. He called it a postmortem examination, which is just a fancy term for looking at a dead body for information and clues. I asked him one of the same questions you just asked me and his response was interesting. He told me some of the same things about his job that I'm going to tell you. He said that he could tell a great deal about a life even after the person dies. He said that bodies tell him stories. Some reveal lives of addiction, some wounds of battle, some lives so short that they had no time to be fully defined and fulfilled. Some even reflect obstacles overcome. When he combines the physical story with interviews from the living about the behavioral side, he ends up with a fairly clear picture and definition of the dead person's life. That's not true in every case, but I'm trying to make a point.

"Regarding seeing cold and naked bodies, no, that doesn't bother me either. I treat the body with respect, but it doesn't represent any ghostly or ghastly presence. We are born with nothing and can leave with nothing except our soul, and it's what I believe about that soul that makes me feel good about my job. You know, Buck, we don't just have a soul. We are each a special soul of body, mind, and spirit created by God for the purpose of reflecting who He is. It's this set of beliefs that makes me unafraid of my own death. Someday, when you're ready, I'd love it if you'd ask me about this. I have a lot to add about how God has impacted my life and how He's changed me."

I was actually going to think about his last comments. In the past, I wouldn't have even considered talking about anything spiritual, but with Max, it was different. I saw something in him that was special. At least, if it came up again with him, I wouldn't refuse to talk about it. Instead of thinking only about life as body and mind, maybe I would consider that there really is a soul unique to each human being. My guess is that my thoughts would still lead to a dead end, but maybe it was time to think it through again.

We finished setting up the flowers and I unpacked the urns and got them on the shelf. Most of our remaining time together was spent talking about Harper and Mrs. Hawkins. He loved talking of how "blessed" he was and about "the loves of his life" and "my Lucie". Although I didn't understand anything about "blessings", it was fun for me to see the amount of love in that family. I guess if a funeral director had to bury Mr. Hawkins, it would be pretty easy to see that his life had not been wasted.

Mr. Hawkins paid me the twenty dollars he owed me and gave me a five-dollar tip. He wanted to give me a ride home, but he was just too busy. He said the tip was for good work, but I also believed that it was because he felt guilty about me having to take the bus back to Armourvale.

I was feeling great on the bus ride home and when I got off, I had a burger and fries at Mickey D's. I made a swing by Milo's home and told him a bit about my day and near sunset headed off to my house. I didn't realize it at the time, but I would be seeing Milo sooner than I anticipated.

As I walked the rest of the way to my house, I started doing postmortem exams on some of the living around me. Realizing that this was a contradiction of terms, I wondered what I should call that examination. Maybe that was the business Dr. Guss was in.

CHAPTER ELEVEN
Walking With Weeds

I heard the noises even before I stepped onto the back stairs, and I had a good idea about what I was hearing. Some sounds don't leave much room for interpretation. The quick sequence of sounds also added weight to my conclusions. I heard a hand or fist slap skin, a woman's voice issue a half scream and half yell, followed quickly by the thud of a body hitting the floor. Each sound was distinct but only a single second separated the three. As I reached the back door, dropped Big Red, and ran into the kitchen, I heard a man's voice yelling a long string of cuss words one after the other. Each profane word gurgling from the man's voice ended with the name "Maria." Finally, as I entered the living room, I saw and heard a piece of furniture crash across the room and a glass lamp break.

I saw JJ, on top of my mom, slapping her face back and forth. As all the rage from the past year escaped completely from my other, cavernous world and completely took over, I became a different person. I knew it was my eyes flying through the air towards the scene, but I couldn't tell if my body was attached or not. I saw JJ below me with someone's fists hitting him, but I didn't comprehend what was really happening. As the fists of the unknown flew, my mind noted that I was hearing almost no sound. "Who turned off the sound," a corner of my mind asked? Another part of my mind was yelling, "Hit! Destroy! Save Mom!" My gut was tight with fear, but I didn't know if I was afraid he would hurt me or afraid that I would kill him. In the end, I knew I no longer had control, but was able to realize that it wasn't a dream. As my mind started to process small portions of this out-of-body experience, I realized, "Oh! It's me. Those are my hands!"

At that same moment, in a flash of spinning lights, I heard a sound from inside my head, but it wasn't a voice. It was a crack from a violent blow. I was disoriented again. I looked at the ceiling. I heard a woman's voice yelling. My internal voice was again furiously asking questions. "What is she saying? Why is she yelling? Why am I so dizzy? Who hit me? Oh, my head hurts. Why is warm water running down my neck?"

My mind began to work again and I finally realized that my mom was the one yelling and the one who had hit me over the head. "You really are a jerk. What business do you have sticking your uppity nose into our affairs? You really aren't worth a plug nickel." Her cusses followed, and she continued. "I should let him tear you apart."

As I got part way to my feet, I heard a crack and felt my body break in half. I found myself on my back and couldn't breathe. I looked up to see JJ's face with a maniacal appearance as he stood over me shaking his fists. I kicked up, knocked him back, and jumped to my feet. I stopped. JJ sat on the floor in surprise while Mom was still yelling at full tilt.

Some of her yelling was garbled, but I clearly understood, "Get the hell out of my house and never come back."

"Where is Little Maria," I asked?

Everyone seemed to freeze. I didn't know where the question came from, but there it was, and it led to a short pause in her yelling.

Mom caught her breath and continued. "She's fine, now get out. We've given you everything you ever needed, and look what we get. I never want to see you again. JJ, leave him alone and let him get out."

Her words weren't needed. JJ was standing still with his mouth gaped open and slobber dripping from his chin. Why she thought she could stop him from hitting me when she couldn't make him stop hitting her was a mystery. Maybe, he just didn't want to be kicked again or maybe he had released his rage. Either way, he was no longer in his attack mode. Mom finished her verbal tirade with "Buck", and her ugly finger pointed towards the back door.

Mom's choice and words were clear. Even with the violence and even with the drunkenness, she had chosen JJ over me. Whether viewed as an escape or an expulsion, I was to leave my cell with my life and the few belongings that I could fit into Big Red and carry under my arm.

As I held a towel to my head, I went into my room. I made sure I had all my school items, stuffed a few additional clothes into Big Red, used a belt to tie around a bedroll, and headed out the door. My one free hand still held the towel soaked with blood from the gash on my head.

I had a bad headache and felt dizzy as I took the back steps. My ribs hurt with each breath, but mostly I felt an overwhelming sadness. It was bad enough for my mom to have called me mental, but, in those moments, she had called me unwanted and gone. Regardless of that misery, I felt an odd relief. I was afraid of what was next, the unknown, but knew that I could not continue to stay sane in the midst of insanity. Only two things were certain; I had been expelled and I needed to decide where to go. I had certainly decided, "No turning back!"

Like a horse trained to return home without a touch of the reign, my feet led me to Milo's post. Although my body shook from the events and my mind went into a fog, my feet marched to what seemed like a pre-determined destination. I had been hit before, but I had never been in a fight. As I approached Milo, he swiveled his salvaged executive chair and, with an uncharacteristic move, he stood and watched me approach. As I got closer, he reached out both arms and met me with a hug. He seemed to know what had happened. Maybe he didn't know the details, but he could read my signs as surely as a driver could read a stop sign. I cried. Milo sobbed.

"Buck, I'm so sorry." He asked for no information, no explanation, and he didn't wait for me to ask for an invitation. Milo just said, "Come on, let's get that cleaned up and get you settled. I'll take care of you, Buck, don't worry."

As we passed through the old gate and headed down the trail, neither of us spoke. Yet I felt welcome. In the dimness of a streetlight, even the weeds felt welcoming, and I started to relax. I was sure that one of the famous authors I studied in Lit' class would romanticize this walk with a flowery sentence or two. Their quotation might read: "The weeds stood as shadowed sentries for the camp. These remnants of a season past seemed to have poised positions of purpose unlike the ugly chaos of waste in the place just departed." Regardless, no amount of pretending could make it anything other than a sad walk down a dirty, dark, pathway leading to a group of outcasts that I was about to join.

Still I wondered at my imaginative author and thought, "Are these dead weeds or wildflowers waiting for spring? Either way, they have more life and beauty than the apartment at 622 Cole." As sad and as hurting as I was, I decided that I would rather walk with weeds than live with evil.

Milo moved his reading material off the extra bed and had me stretch out on my side. He cleaned my wound, put some antibiotic cream on the cut, and told me that what he was going to do next might hurt a little. He took small segments of my hair from each side of the one-inch gash and pulled each hair segment towards the other. As he did, he pulled the two sides of the cut skin together and then double-tied the hair as tightly as he could.

"This should heal up real nicely over the next week or so. This isn't the first cut I've fixed up in this camp. I've become somewhat of an expert. Now, we just need to keep it clean and keep some antiseptic cream on it. You should only end up with a little scar. No one should even notice it, unless you become bald in your old age. What do you think of that, Buck Ol'Boy?"

"Thanks Milo. I didn't know where else to go or what to do. I'll try to figure out something, but I can't go back to my house."

"Buck, I've said this before. You are welcome here anytime and welcome for as long as you need. I'll tell the patrol boys tonight that you are here, just in case your mom tries to make trouble for you. I doubt that she will. I think Officer Whales is on tonight. He's a good man. We can trust him. We'll just take one day at a time."

Milo gave me a bottle of water. While I drank, he made me take my shirt off and he cleaned up the blood on my neck and back. He also took my shirt and used another bottle of water to rinse it off. He hung the wet shirt over a narrow white rope that hung across one corner of the tent.

As Milo worked away on my shirt and while I snacked on an energy bar, Milo started mumbling and seemed to be slowly working his way into a fury. I knew he wasn't talking to me, but I also wasn't sure he was talking to himself. At first, I thought maybe he was just mumbling words of anger, but I finally concluded that he was mumbling an angry prayer.

I caught some of his words, "I've known some dysfunctional families before, but these people take the cake. They are not just dysfunctional and destructive, but they are despicable and dangerous and evil. It makes me wonder how forgiveness and redemption can ever apply. Lord, you will need to tell me what I'm supposed to do on this. You know what I want to do, so you need to give me an option. Okay, I'll wait."

I couldn't help myself. I decided to feed Milo some of his own words. "Hey Milo, what was it you said the other day? Oh, I know. It was, 'Bad isn't good and most bad has no good reason, but sometimes out of bad can come good.' Did I get that right?

With a harrumph, he cleared his throat, stepped quickly out of the tent, spit, stepped back in just as quickly and said, "Look. That was a private conversation. Now, just shut up and get some sleep. We'll talk about this tomorrow." Although he smiled a slight smile, I kept my mouth shut.

I finished my drink and snack, unrolled my bedding, took two aspirin, and tried to sleep. I was able to sleep on and off, but odd sounds and odd thoughts kept waking me at various intervals.

During one of those later waking moments, my head and ribs hurt so badly that I took two more aspirin and drank another bottle of water. I peeked out the tent, saw a slight bit of light on the eastern horizon, and went right back to bed. I started shaking from being cold and wrapped myself back in my blankets. I quickly stopped shaking. Within thirty minutes or so, my headache eased and I started to drift back to sleep.

It was nice to have medicine for the physical pain that JJ and Mom had caused, but one of my last thoughts, before going back to sleep, was to wonder if Milo had a way to ease the other hurt; the pain inflicted by Mom's words and from Mom's choice. I realized that wasn't Milo's responsibility anymore than it was his responsibility to provide a bed or an aspirin. Maybe I should try my own private conversation with Milo's higher power and ask, "So, whose job is it anyway to heal my heart?" In spite of my unanswered question, I slept well for another few hours.

When I woke up, I panicked for a moment. That last bit of sleep was so sound that I had to re-orient myself. My mind asked, "Where am I? What day is it?" The answers came quickly, but the answers also brought with them a flood of more information than I had asked for. I lay on the bed for a few minutes going back over the events. At first the memories made me tense, but as I lay there and listened, I started to feel myself relax. I heard the birds, the breeze through the trees, a train, and someone scraping the grill outside the tent. I looked at Milo's bed. It was empty. He was fixing breakfast. My head felt okay. I was still angry and hurt, but I wasn't afraid. I thought, "Home should be a place where one isn't afraid."

As I pulled on my Wolverine boots, I flipped open the tent flap and stepped outside. Milo looked me over with a serious and concerned up and down assessment. Before he said anything, he ducked into the tent and came right back out with a coat and a baseball cap. "Here, put these on. These are extra. We will go to the Goodwill Store tomorrow and get you a few things. I'm fixin' some campfire biscuits and coffee. Hope that's okay."

"Absolutely. Sounds great. Thanks Milo. If you want, I've got some money and could run over to McDonald's."

"No, I don't need that for now. If you need something extra after a while, you can run over." Milo got the folding chairs and we sat and talked some, but mostly just watched the sun and listened to nature.

"Buck, I don't need to know all the details about last night and probably don't want to know everything, but I'm here for you to talk to about it and for you to share what you're able to share." Milo paused to let that sink in and then he continued.

"I've learned that it's good to get feelings out on the table, so to speak. A person can only keep 'em in so long, and if you get too many of them built up, they are liable to erupt. You might remember what I told you before about how hurt and anger can look a lot alike with the only difference being who they are aimed at when they do erupt. Well, the only way you can keep them from exploding is to get them out, share them early on with someone who will really listen and who really cares. So, if you are able to talk, I've got time to listen. I thought I'd skip church today since I ain't shaved or nothin'." He let out a hardy laugh. I liked to hear him laugh.

I did share. I told him all. I talked for the next hour as we ate a pile of biscuits and drank the rotten coffee. As I spoke, I got hurt and mad and afraid all over again. In the end, however, it was good. Milo had certainly listened, heard, and understood. He even started mumbling again.

His listening took off some of the weight I felt. It was good. I felt that I had escaped the chaos of the night and was, instead, occupying a place of sanity and order, even if it was in a homeless camp. It was good.

"Milo, you have to be one of the wisest men alive. You seem to know just what to do and say. Whether it's fixing my head or just shutting up and listening, you are one of a kind. I would never have thought that a kid like me could have a grownup as one of my best friends."

"Well, I beg to differ about part of your comment. I admit, I have some good information and insights, but I don't count myself as wise. Wisdom is a whole different ballgame than information. Someone who is wise is able to apply their insights and conclusions and not just recite them. Wisdom may begin with a person speaking about understandings gained from critical experiences, but wisdom can only be claimed when that person exhibits enough courage to apply that understanding. At least for me, courage and wisdom seem to be inseparable partners. Up to now, I've shared the insights, but I've been slightly short on the courage end." He let out another gifted laugh.

Milo took a long break from talking, but eventually picked it up again. "I'll know in the next few months if I have any courage. Maybe then I'll let you use the word wise."

Milo shared that he was gradually trying to gather up some of the broken pieces in his life and put things either back together or to, at least, put them back into some kind of order. He had a girlfriend who owned a house near the Med Center. He had known her most of his life and had gone to high school with her. Their connection continued during his days of practicing law. Milo related that he lost track of her at some point, especially after he closed his office. The two then reconnected at an AA meeting six months ago. As they visited after AA meetings, they realized that they had gone through similar life experiences and a romantic relationship quickly developed. Luckily, she didn't have to fall as far as he had before she, in Milo's terms, "got sober."

DeAnn allowed Milo to have his mail sent to her home, for him to keep some important papers at her house, and, recently, had even allowed Milo to come over and use a room in the house to do some paid work for an attorney. Milo wasn't yet practicing law again, but he was preparing all kinds of papers for the attorney to review and finalize. Milo also occasionally used DeAnn's place to clean up and had slept on the floor a few nights when the temperatures were sub-zero. He liked DeAnn a great deal and thought they had a future together, but they both had decided to take their time with the relationship and make sure they "had their heads on straight".

He described DeAnn as the perfect listener and hoped that the relationship came together, "and soon."

"Buck, talking to someone can make life tolerable, but only when talking to someone who cares enough to hear through the noise of confusion. DeAnn is that person for me. When I finish talking with her, it's like I've finished an incredible meal followed by a huge bowl of Peanut Butter Panic Ice Cream. There's nothing better. Mmm."

"Harper makes me feel the same way."

Milo ended his sharing with, "If we prove our worth together this summer, I might just be moving out of this hotel. Then, just maybe, you can call me wise."

At the end of Milo's update, I needed to visit my friends, the weeds, to allow for some of the coffee to make a clean getaway. It was good.

CHAPTER TWELVE
A Deadly Choice

Sunday really was a day of rest. Milo took me to DeAnn's house. Although I had heard Milo mention her name a few times in the past few months, I had never connected the dots. The realization that he had a serious relationship with her made me recognize how little I had been listening to him.

As I was formally introduced, it became clear that Milo had previously told DeAnn all about me. Immediately after the introduction, he told her about the previous night and JJ's attack on my mom, and her reaction to my attempted rescue. She didn't say anything at first. She looked at me for a minute, shook her head, and then waved me over to her.

"Here, let me look at that head of yours." She checked on Milo's job of "hair stitching" and found it to be quite good. I asked her if she could help with camouflaging the wound for school. She tried to comb the hair over, but her efforts didn't work very well. Milo and I looked at each other when she mentioned, "comb over", and laughed as we thought back to the Knock, Knock joke with Harper. DeAnn, of course, didn't get it, and it would have taken too long to tell her, so we got right back to the issue of how to hide the wound. She asked me if I could wear a hat in the hallways and just take it off as classes started. I couldn't think of a better idea.

DeAnn made me feel totally welcome. She allowed me to take a shower and fed me a hot meal of spaghetti and meatballs with a side of garlic toast. It reminded me of the last time I had a home cooked meal at Corina's home. It was interesting that I thought I knew most of what there was to know about Milo, but the fullness of his life with DeAnn was his special secret, and special she was. For someone in her late forties or early fifties, she was also a knockout. Seeing them together seemed to mock mathematics as one plus one appeared to equal a third and different one.

As we talked over dinner and as I did a load of laundry, she let several other secrets out of the bag as well. It seemed that Milo had once been a better lawyer than he let on and was once considered judge material.

DeAnn was surprisingly truthful and open about her being a recovering alcoholic and shared some of her life's "tribulations" as she called them. One of those events had been her divorce. DeAnn's ex-husband had also been an attorney, and she had been her ex's main staff person. "Michael and I have been friends for a long time, even before my divorce."

I couldn't get used to anyone calling Milo, Michael. Regardless of the name issue, being around the two of them that day was nearly perfect and exactly what I needed. I was so comfortable that I felt like I'd entered a peaceful but alien world. In some ways I was sorry that the day ended, but I also wanted to get back to school on Monday.

Considering all that was going on, school went extremely well that next day. I was surprised. I was self-conscious about the injury to my head, but the hat worked well. My classes and grades were in great shape. The biggest problem was what wasn't there: Harper. She was still doing her schoolwork from home with the help of a tutor and going to a speech therapist for an hour a day, six days a week. Although Harper wasn't around, I was able to spend some time with Corina, and I gave her all the gory details about Saturday night. I told her that she could share it all with Harper, but that I didn't want her to tell anyone else. I needed to trust someone and Corina and Harper were totally trustworthy. I might also need their help in figuring out some long-term plans. I just couldn't think very far ahead as I approached this unknown territory.

I told Corina that I would catch Mrs. Sheppard up before the end of the week if my head looked better. I planned to tell her that I would be staying with friends for a few days and would ask her not to call my mom's Trac phone at my house. Well, my old house or ex-house or whatever it was. Again, I didn't have all of that thought out either, but, like Milo said, "you need to take one day at a time."

A DEADLY CHOICE

On Monday after school, Milo met me at Manny's around 4:30. We had just enough time for him to walk me to the Goodwill Store. With only twenty dollars, we picked up three sets of clothing, socks, underwear and all. With the three sets I had salvaged from my house, I was in great shape when it came to clothing. I was only short one set of parents, but they were out of stock. Of course, Milo's goodwill was sufficient for the time being.

On Tuesday after school, I again worked at Manny's. Before I started work, Manny allowed me to use the phone, and I called Harper. She was mad that I hadn't come over or called during all of this. We talked for thirty minutes until Manny interrupted by handing me a broom. I got the message, told Harper, and she ended the conversation with a sweet request, "Please, Buck, call me every night and come by as soon as you can. I need you to comb over hair and give me a kiss," and she giggled.

As I worked, Little Maria came in. That was a first. Even more out of character, she asked if she could talk with me in private.

"Buckie, I don't know what to do. Momma and JJ are acting crazy. They are just mad all the time and drinking all the time, and JJ's starting to hassle me. Sometimes, I'm afraid. The other night I was in behind my bed and didn't come out all night except for once, when I just couldn't hold it any longer. What do you think I should do?"

"I don't know Lil." I had never liked her being called Little Maria.

"What do you mean about JJ hassling you?" Her answer was vague and she seemed to not want to say more on that.

"You may have to do what I did for a while. Make your room your own hideout."

"Let me think about this, and do me a favor. Drop by here after school whenever I'm working. That way you can always let me know the latest. Here, let me give you some treats to have in your room. Also, don't forget to keep all your school stuff and backpack in the room with you so that you kinda' have your own little house in there. Do you understand?"

"Yes." She took the treats and stuffed them into her purple backpack.

"I thought of one more thing, Lil. If Mom is ever in a good mood, ask her if you can use my old room. My room has the window by the porch and is close to the back door. If you have that room, you could make a quick getaway if things get really ugly. I'm at Milo's, but don't tell anyone. If you really need me, I'll be there." Lil gave me a quick hug and was off.

As I stood and watched Lil walk down the street, I realized that our conversation was the first real exchange in the past year involving anything but "hello". I couldn't even remember the last one. I had never felt much for her, because I assumed she didn't want to have any association with me, or anyone in that house. Yet, at that moment, I felt sorry for her and even felt some guilt. I also felt mad. Her fear and her request for help had given me one more reason to hate JJ. I had to fight a thought that I wished I had hurt him, badly.

When I got back to camp, I told Milo. He said, "I think we need to think seriously about this. As much as you don't want to Buck, we may need to consider letting the welfare department in on all of this. Your mom and JJ are making some sick choices and those choices are putting more and more people at risk. I promised you that I would never contact welfare without your permission, but, now, we need to consider her. If she shows up with any bruises, or if JJ is trying to mess with her in other ways, we may need to bite the bullet and turn his sorry ass in. Don't you think?"

"Yeah, you're probably right, Milo. Let's see how the week goes." I needed to think as well. Getting protective services involved may send JJ over the top and get someone really hurt. Plus, I'm still worried that Mom or JJ could make up some lie to tell Summit and get me kicked out of there and into a regular school.

I needed to think the problem through, but all I could really think and mutter was, "Damn, they are pathetic. I hate them both."

I had picked up an old Sunday newspaper at Manny's, and Milo was enjoying reading one section while I had another. I came to the obituary section and started reading some of them. I wanted to compare those to the one about Mrs. Daugherty that I read at the funeral home. I found a strange fascination with them and especially liked looking at the ones with pictures and the ones with odd, old-time names. Even with that, they surely couldn't be doing justice to the lives of any of the people listed. I was still left wondering about each.

I actually started making fun of some of the items included in the obits. "Milo, listen to this one. This guy lists that he was a member of AARP. What do you have to do to be a member of AARP except reach a

A DEADLY CHOICE

certain age?" I asked, but knew the answer. "Do you think that's the most significant meaning he had in life?" Again, I didn't expect an answer. I started making fun of other things, but Milo finally had heard enough.

"Buck, I know you are just wondering, but, without knowing those people, you just can't make any judgment about their lives. "

I got irritated, "Okay. So just how do we know if a life has been worthwhile?"

"Well, Buck, I wonder if you are asking that about others or if you are asking about yourself. If you are really asking about yourself, and I think you are, you need to start asking about yourself and stop making fun of others. I realize that you are impatient to find out the exact and full meaning of your life, but sometimes that's a discovery process and not a single answer matter." Milo smiled, but he was also confronting me a bit about how insensitive and how judgmental I was being. He was also telling me to be patient, but I was not at a patient point in my life. I felt that I needed an answer soon, or, at least a partial answer.

Milo added, "Who knows, maybe your purpose in life is to protect Little Maria."

"Damn it, Milo. I don't need a guilt trip." I tossed the paper down and went to the weeds.

The rest of that week went well. Lil dropped by the store on the days I worked. The plan for her to retreat to her room as often as possible seemed to be working. She did, however, indicate that JJ and Mom were still drinking heavily each night. I wondered where the money was coming from, but neither Lil nor I knew the answer to that. She did say that Mom wasn't opening the mail any longer, so I assumed bills weren't getting paid.

I went to bed early Saturday evening, but very early that Sunday morning, I was awakened by an unusual sound. I heard voices outside the tent. I squinted at Milo's bed and saw that it was empty. I realized that one of the voices outside was Milo's. I also heard a sound that, at first, sounded like a bird pecking on the tarp.

Listening more closely, I realized it was light rain. "Milo, what are you doing in the rain?"

Milo came up close to the tent flap and softly says, "I'll be right in, just hold on."

The two men had one last interchange and the tent flap swung open. Milo and the other man entered. Milo turned on a camping light revealing a uniformed police officer who had to stand at least six foot four and who had hands as big as footballs. As I looked up at this imposing figure, I thought to myself, "Oh, crap. Mom has turned me in as a runaway. The jig is up. My future is toast."

"Buck, this is Officer Whales. You've probably heard me talk about him. He's come to talk to you about JJ and your Mom."

I swung my feet to the carpeted floor of the tent, brushed my hair back, and tried to get totally awake so I could focus. Even knowing it was no solution, I was tempted to run past Whales and out the door, but I didn't. I couldn't have gotten past him anyway.

I thought to myself, "Ok, no getting around it. Here it comes."

My voice was clearly defensive as I blurted out, "So, what about them? She's the one who kicked me out!"

Milo quickly shot back with, "We all know that Buck, that's not what this is about."

The rain outside picked up. I didn't consider it a hard rain, just a more persistent drip. Still, the sound on the tarp, my sleepy feeling, and the dim light made it a dream-like setting.

I tried to shake myself awake as Officer Whales, who was crouching to keep his head from hitting the ceiling, started talking in a deep voice. "Milo is right Buck. It's about something that happened a couple of hours ago. Your mom was involved in a car accident off the Belt Highway. She was a passenger." He paused and seemed to study me.

"A man was driving by the name of Jesse. It looks like he had been drinking and speeding. The light rain made the street slick and the car hit a utility pole." Again, he stopped talking for a moment, moved to one knee in front of me, and picked his verbal report back up.

"Buck, I'm afraid that your mom didn't make it." He stopped again, to give me time to react. My guess was that most kids would have broken down at that point, but I was stoic. I didn't know what I felt.

The three of us stood there for the moment. I had a strange thought before I started peppering the officer with questions. My first thought was, "I kinda' like the sound of the rain, it's peaceful." I knew it was an out-of-place thought, but it slipped in there none the less. Then I started with my questions. I think I surprised the officer with my line of questioning as it wasn't about my mom or JJ.

"Officer, do you know where my little sister is?"

"No. We went by your apartment, but got no answer."

"So, what happened to JJ, I mean Jesse?"

"He was injured, but not badly. He was lucky. The car was nearly sliced in half, but the impact was on your mom's side. The driver's area was hardly touched. She also didn't appear to be wearing her seatbelt. We took Jesse to the Med Center to get cleared. As soon as he gets medically cleared and as soon as we draw blood to confirm that he was drinking, he's going to jail. He could be charged with anything up to and including vehicular homicide."

I tried to let the officer's entire report soak in, but I just couldn't wrap my head around anything. I couldn't sort out my feelings, I had no logical process in mind, and I was overwhelmed with the unknown. "What am I supposed to do?"

"Well, what we usually do is notify all the family members, and we want to make sure that the minors, uh, the kids are properly taken care of. Who would you like us to contact?"

I thought quickly. That could be a trick question. If I answered that one wrong, I may end up in a foster home. I didn't know where my dad was. My guess was that he had gone back to Mexico. "Think, Buck, think," I kept telling myself.

Milo was silent and gave me just enough time to blurt out, "Well, my dad's out of town, but I'm sure when he comes back, Little Maria and I can stay with him. We have no grandparents or, if we do, they aren't around. We do have some great friends, and we could stay with them for the next couple of days. Would that be OK?"

My statement had some truth in it, but the message sent was a lie, and I knew it. Milo knew it too, but must have been thinking along my lines.

Officer Whales thought my comments over for a moment, nodded his head in agreement, but added, "I'll have to let dispatch know, and I may have to call your friends to confirm. Also, I'll need to put their names down on the report. If it was just you, I could probably get by and let you stay here with Milo, but I'll need to put down where to find Maria. Do you think your friends would mind if I called them now?"

"I think that would be fine, but would you let me make the call and then you talk to them?" I didn't want Mr. Hawkins spilling the beans about my dad.

"Sure. So, who are you going to call?"

"It's a family named Hawkins, the dad runs a funeral home."

"Oh, I know Max. The PD works with him all the time. That's a great resource. How do you know that family?"

As the officer handed me his cell phone, I responded while I dialed. "Well, I go to school with their daughter, Harper, and I did some part time work for him just recently." I left out the details.

I called. I knew that Max was used to getting calls at night, but this one probably caught him off guard. I didn't realize how upset I was until I started talking. It took ten minutes of conversation just to explain things and a bit longer before I was able to ask him to let Maria stay. Of course, I didn't detail everything. I told him I'd only been visiting Milo.

On his own, Max readily agreed to a short stay, and he said that he would discuss other plans with Lucie. He also agreed to call Mr. and Mrs. Schuler and give them an update. He said that he would stay up and wait for us, but I told him that it would be mid-day before we got there. I explained that we needed to go to the apartment, find Lil, and get some of her stuff together. I explained that we would stay at the apartment the rest of that night.

I knew the Hawkins family went to church on Sunday, so I told him. "I'll call around noon and, if Lil and I can't get a ride, you can pick us up then." All was agreed.

I handed the phone back to Officer Whales and Mr. Hawkins gave him the required information. I thought all was lost when the Officer said, "This is really nice of you to help out until the dad gets back." Yet, somehow, Mr. Hawkins didn't respond or ask more. Maybe, he had been caught off guard and was still processing all of the events just like the rest of us.

The phone call must have triggered unknown emotions. I realized that I was crying. I didn't want to cry. I didn't think my tears were out of sadness as much as out of fear and anxiety. Either way, I had to admit to myself that tears were running down my cheeks. Others didn't seem to notice. The teardrops appeared on my face and then disappeared on the muddy ground as though they were just additional raindrops.

In the midst of my wondering about tears, Milo startled me by putting his arm on my shoulder and saying, "I think that's a great plan, Buck. Good job."

Milo turned back to the Officer. "Whales, Buck and I will go back to the apartment. Buck knows how to get in even if it's locked. Maria might even be there. She may have been afraid to answer the door."

I regrouped, refocused, and chimed in with, "Right. A loud knock would have scared her. Also, I told her to use her room as a hideout from JJ. She might be in there just hanging out listening to her music. Let's go Milo."

Thinking ahead, Milo asked Whales if he could use his phone to call DeAnn. She quickly answered and Milo gave her an update. The call ended as Milo said he'd call her the next morning.

While Milo was on the phone with DeAnn, Officer Whales asked about my reference to "hideout from JJ", but I just told him that JJ had been drunk a lot lately and was just being a jerk. It didn't seem necessary to open another can of worms that night.

Milo fished out a couple of umbrellas from one of the boxes below his bed; we walked up the trail, and jumped into the back seat of the patrol car. Arriving at the apartment, Officer Whales offered to come in. We told him that we would take it from there.

He wasn't chased off that easily though and said, "Well, you go up and make sure she really is there. If she is, give me a wave and I'll get back in service. If she's not, I'm going to stick around. Oh, by the way, Buck. In case you're wondering or in case anyone asks, it looks like your mom didn't feel a thing."

His last comment stopped me for a moment and I looked at him with confusion. I started to say something in return, but my brain locked up. I couldn't reduce my thoughts to words, especially those about Mom's ability to feel and regarding the details of the crash. It was another point in life where no sentence came, so I simply said, "Oh, okay. Thanks." I re-focused and bounded up the steps two steps at a time.

I gave a holler as I came in the back door. "Lil, it's OK. It's just me, Buck. It's safe, JJ's not here." I knocked on the door of her room and peeked in. Sure enough, Lil was in her room. Her head popped up from the side of the bed and she smiled.

Milo waved off Whales. He waved back and took off.

Lil was concerned with seeing me, but not because she thought something was wrong. "What are you doing here, Buck. If JJ or Mom catch you here, you're gonna' be dead meat. They might be back any minute."

"Lil, Milo and I have to tell you something that's going to be hard to listen to. Mom and JJ were in a wreck tonight. She and JJ won't be coming back."

Milo and I took turns sharing information. We told Lil all that we knew. She cried the whole time. I didn't know any more about where her feelings were coming from than I knew about my own. I was sure she was afraid of the unknown too. I knew for sure that she wasn't upset about JJ going to jail.

I wondered if sometimes we cry because we think we are supposed to cry. Again, I had no way of knowing.

Lil and I talked for the next hour. Much of that hour's conversation was spent wishing that Mom had never met JJ and that she had not started drinking again. For the hour after that, I told her to get some of her most important things together. I found an old suitcase and laid it on her bed, told her to pick out a few complete outfits, and asked her to put those and her personal items into the luggage. If they didn't fit, just give me a holler. She hollered fairly soon and complained that all of her CDs wouldn't fit. I modified her priorities, gave her a paper sack, and finally got her treasures ready.

Over that entire two-hour period, Milo was sitting at a table going through papers. He asked me, "Buck, did your Mom ever talk about a will?"

"You've got to be kidding, Milo. Mom never even planned a meal, much less planned for her death. I don't think she even owns anything to list in a will."

Milo made a few noises in his throat, but eventually came out with what he was thinking. "Well, I've handled a lot of estates and I've learned to expect the unexpected. I'm also just trying to think ahead about how we deal with the custody issue. Let's come back tonight or tomorrow and sort through some of this."

"Well, you're not going to find anything important. I'll guarantee you this, nothing exists beyond what we see right here in front of us."

I looked at the calendar. It was still very early in the morning of April 26th, another Sunday. I realized that this would not be a day of rest for any of us, unless I considered my mom at rest. I decided to think about that later.

CHAPTER THIRTEEN
Keep It Simple

After an hour of talking and after periods of crying, Lil finally fell asleep on her bed as I patted her back. I think she may have considered that, at that moment, I was the only person in the world who understood anything about her. Before sleeping, Lil had asked a number of questions and most of them covered some part of, "What's going to happen to me now?"

Her asking questions and wondering about the next step gave me comfort. I thought maybe she and I had something in common after all. Of course, her questions didn't wander as far into the unknown as mine, at least, not yet. I told myself to give her a break. She's only twelve.

In answering her immediate concerns, "Where will I sleep" and "Who will feed me?" I explained that she would temporarily stay with Harper. That response seemed to give her some comfort, and she eventually dozed off. Still, her questions still went unanswered about any longer-term plans. I had some of the same questions, but mine included several deeper concerns. I knew these other deeper questions existed somewhere in the back of my mind, but I couldn't seem to form all of them into words that made any sense.

As I listened to Lil sleep, I wondered about life and death. As thoughts darted through my head, a few questions took shape. Would Mom have an obituary? If she did, what would it say? Was there any meaning to her life to list? Would Little Maria and I be listed before JJ? What would I say if I had to write an obituary? Who would I say she was?

My thoughts went on to other questions that had implications for Lil and me alike. These took a circuit something like: Did Little Maria and I inherit anything besides our body from her? If she had or has a spirit, where did it come from and where did it go? Who are we today, now that we have neither a mother nor a father around? Do relationships exist then end at death without meaning? Should I feel guilty about hating her and did that have anything to do with her death?

I finally gave up, shrugged, and told myself, "Well, at least one thing is clear. I've got my mind and I've got Big Red. That's my inheritance. Yes, and a fine one it is. The rest can wait another day." After putting my questions to bed, I slept for a couple of hours. My questions, though, never rested very long. I knew I'd be asking many more in the days to come.

I don't think Milo slept at all. Around 6:30, when I came out of Lil's room, Milo was seated at a table that he had cleaned off. He had papers and envelops stacked in ten to twelve different piles, and he was in the middle of going through a large, old, shoebox full of papers. Mom's papers had never been organized.

The shoebox especially intrigued me. "Where did you find that box Milo, and what's in it?"

Milo was studying several items and never looked up as he responded with carefully measured words, "Got it from a closet in your mom's bedroom. Don't know what all is in it yet. I've just started to look through it. It looks like several types of important papers are here. So far, I see birth certificates that I'm going to pull out and take with us, and it looks to have papers connected with where she worked. What did she do at the Wright Plant?"

"I'm not really sure exactly. I know she did factory work and made things like ice cream cartons. She probably still has a job there. I think she was on temporary leave for hurting her hand in one of the machines. I don't really believe it was hurt as badly as she let on, but she was still getting some kind of paycheck. Why are you asking?"

"Oh, I'll need to have someone study this situation more than I can right now, but several of these items could be important, especially if she had any retirement fund or life insurance through work. You were right about me not finding a will, but you may be wrong about her not having anything.

"Also, there was some mail on the kitchen counter addressed to Jesse. One envelope looks like it's from an insurance company. I'm not going to open his mail, but if he had insurance on his car, it opens up another possibility for funds. I know how to find that out. Also, if he is charged with a crime related to the wreck, we may have another route to go. I don't need to get into the details now, but, come Monday or Tuesday, I'll have Ed Casey, the attorney I work for, check on a couple of things for us. Is that OK with you?"

"Sure, do what you want on that."

"Buck, we will also need to talk about some other legal issues. You are really too young to have to deal with them, but when we get to the Hawkins' house later today, would you mind if we brought them into a conversation about things such as a funeral and getting temporary custody papers on you and Lil?"

"That makes sense to me. The Hawkins could really help. I know we need to plan something. Let's do it. I would think Max has seen about everything, and Lucie and Harper are so special that I'd love for them to be in on it. You know we could also see if my friend Corina could have her parents over, in addition. They really helped me out when Harper was in the hospital and in rehab.

"Milo, you need to do what you think is right, because I'm more out of it than with it. I'm pretty overwhelmed."

"I would find it odd if you felt any other way. Hey Buck, how about I clean up the kitchen a little and see if I can find something to eat? I'm hungry."

"You go ahead. If it smells good, I might come out, but I'd like to spend some time in my old room, if you don't mind."

Milo put a hand up. "Got it. I'm on my own."

I thought I could go into my old cell just to relax and think some things through, but surprisingly, I fell asleep for another hour.

I smelled sausage or bacon or something like that cooking. As I slowly opened my eyes, it took me a good ten minutes to let my mind catch up to where I was and to go over the events that had returned me to this personal room of reminders.

Even with the smell of the cooking food, I didn't want to leave my room. It had been transformed from cell to sanctuary. In the past, I would have jumped at the chance to get out of my prison, especially when JJ and Mom weren't around, but opening that door at that moment meant opening up to face a day full of unknowns, full of questions, full of tough decisions, and full of confusing emotions. The sudden change of perspective was startling.

I felt a panic attack coming on and tried to remember what Mrs. Sheppard had told me when I felt this way, but my mind raced ahead and wouldn't allow for braking. Opening the door meant facing the facts, as adults would say, but to me, when it came to death, there were no certainties and no facts to face except the one that was obvious. Mom was dead. Stepping outside this shelter meant facing past and present with no sense to be made of either. No sense, only demons. My fears took over. I didn't want to face anything. I wanted to see Harper but even that thought made me worry. If I could just see her it would probably be fine. On the other hand, seeing her would more than likely expose other emotions and dig up more than a grave.

"Stop it, Buck!" I heard my voice whispering instructions over my panic. "Get it together." I tried to think again about Mrs. Sheppard's advice. "What was it? She said something about simple and calm. Oh, I remember. Take the one, obvious, simple next step. Take one little step at a time." Mrs. Sheppard had told me that my mind didn't work like most kids' minds and that my IQ sometimes caused me to over-think and lose track of the obvious. She called it paralysis by analysis.

Mrs. Sheppard was right. "Stop it! Think! Simple!"

My voice didn't whisper the next sentence, it yelled. "So, where is the simple in my life today, God? Just look at what you've done." I meant to ask that question to the absent Mrs. Sheppard, but "God" came out. If God didn't exist, then why was I blaming him? "Stop it! Keep it simple!"

I rubbed my hands back and forth with a nervous motion. "Ok, the most simple thing to do is to sit here and not open the door, but that's really not an option."

Milo yelled through the door. "Hey, Buck. Sounds like you're awake. Why don't you come out and have some breakfast. I just fixed something simple, but I think it should taste great. We need to eat something first and just take this big day as it comes. What do you think Buck?"

I decided to try breakfast. I opened the door as I wondered about the timing of his word, "simple".

Milo said, "Well, how ya' doing?"

"Fine. Doing fine. Yeah, doing OK. I'm hungry. This looks good. Thanks." Intelligent or not, I realized that I was nothing more than a babbling, overwhelmed, fifteen year old kid who, along with a little sister, had just lost another parent. I stared at the plate piled with food. "Milo, what are we eating?"

"Have you never had biscuits and gravy?"

Milo sat down with me and bowed his head. I just stared at him. Finally, I couldn't help but ask him. "Okay, so what did you just pray about?"

"Oh, it was a simple prayer for courage for the day, and to help me just take it one step at a time. Most days that's my prayer and most days that's all I can handle."

I shook my head at what must surely have been coincidental wording but said nothing. We ate in silence. It was good.

Shortly after breakfast, we heard some noise in front of the apartment building. As I looked out the front window and across the large concrete porch area, I noticed a television news truck parking. The noise was the beeping of the truck backing into position. The truck then raised a large, antenna-like structure. A cameraman was unloading gear as a TV reporter talked on her cell phone. After I pulled the shades closed, I cracked open a window to hear what they were saying.

After only about ten minutes, someone knocked on our door. Milo instructed Lil and me not to open it. Lil had just awakened and was eating some of Milo's wonderful biscuit and sausage gravy. She had never had it either.

When we didn't answer the repeated knocks, the reporter went to the apartment below. The neighbors answered and agreed to step out for an interview.

I couldn't hear everything, but I was surprised at what I could hear. The neighbor lady, who was speaking, who I'd never even met, and who I'd never seen with my mom, said, "Oh, she was just the nicest lady. She was just a normal, everyday, hard-working mother. It's just so sad. We're really going to miss her. Well, I don't know anything about all that, but I'm sure her family will miss her."

"What a crock. That's just wrong," I said to no one in particular. I wondered why anyone would say things that they knew nothing about.

After breakfast, Milo insisted that Lil and I help clean up the kitchen. "I like to leave things better than I found them."

I thought that was a good attitude, but wondered why we should clean up some of Mom's messes as well as ours. I like my things neat, but it was hard for me to consider cleaning someone else's grime. Besides, it probably wouldn't be long before the apartment owner would kick us out. Yet, it was probably a good thought and the right thing to do. It looked like Milo was into cleaning up a lot in his life. I wondered if I would be required to change any of my thinking or habits.

When we finished the cleaning, we all stood around and felt some pride in our work. Milo then announced, "On to the next item of the day." Lil and I looked at him with puzzled looks, and he smiled. It was good to see a smile.

Milo directed me to sneak out the back, avoid any reporters that might still be around, go to Manny's, and call DeAnn. He needed her to pick us up at Manny's around eleven, allow us to come to her place and clean up, and then take us over to the Hawkins' home. He wanted to show up around 1:00 in the afternoon so as not to disturb their lunch. That would also allow the whole afternoon for "planning" as Milo put it.

I was out the back and up the alley before anyone in front could have heard the door slam. This was easy and simple. No thinking was required. I needed a task like that.

When I returned, I told Milo that I was successful in reaching DeAnn. With that, he stuffed some key papers into a sack, locked up the apartment, headed out the back, and we met DeAnn as planned.

As soon as we arrived at her house, Milo called Max and confirmed details for the day. We took our time with showers and cleaning up. For me, the shower felt like more than cleaning up, and I knew that I took longer than the others. In fact, I stayed in until I had used all of the remaining hot water. The shower felt like the half time of an important game. I wanted to just stay in it and avoid the second half. The afternoon seemed filled with too many unknowns, and I wasn't sure I could handle them.

After we finished showering and cleaning up, we devoured the ham and cheese sandwiches that DeAnn had fixed. Milo also took some time to sit down and make some notes. I wasn't sure what he was writing, but it, obviously, was in preparation for the afternoon. In one sense, watching him write made me nervous. I wondered what it all meant. On the other hand, it gave me a sense of security. It was good to have someone like him doing things that were designed to help Lil and me. I knew he cared and I knew that we were going to meet with others who cared. That was special, but I was still nervous. I wondered how it was all going to play out.

When Milo finished taking notes and after one final review, we headed out the door. As we did, I noticed that Milo had shaved and was dressed in slacks. I mentioned to Milo, "Hey, you actually look normal." He gave me a mock sneer and a finger point and said, "Don't ever use that word again. Remember, you're the one who said we can't define normal." We both had a good laugh and the laugh seemed to break some of my tension.

As I rode in the back seat towards the Hawkins' home, I thought to myself that a good laugh, a good meal, and a hot shower at the right time can seem like cold drinks in the desert. I felt refreshed, renewed, and even somewhat relaxed. I had only had to yell at myself a couple of times. "Stop it. Keep it simple."

The next simple step is to hug Harper, if she'll let me. "Hey, Milo. Do you know of any good jokes that I can tell Harper?"

CHAPTER FOURTEEN
Closed Casket – Opened Doors

Milo didn't come up with any jokes for me to tell Harper, but that was about the only thing that he didn't do that afternoon at Harper's home. He was a master at leading the group discussion. He also had information and important contacts related to a broad range of issues. Milo wasn't back to practicing law, but he was certainly practicing being an incredibly gifted person who was willing to do the right things and to help the group make great choices.

As I watched my homeless friend interact with all these other people who had also become my friends, I was especially proud of him. At times, I thought to myself that he was more of a parent figure than anyone had ever been. Each of the adults told him how appreciative they were and each said "thank you" more than once. He was humble in each response and said that everyone had offered as much as he did. That was true, but he kept the group focused and was able to give us an idea of what might be possible, especially in the legal realm. Max, of course, had all the bases covered when it came to the funeral issues.

Harper greeted me royally, and I got my hug. That, however, was about all the attention I received. Following the initial "hello" and hug, Harper's focus centered on Lil. I didn't get it. It must have been a girl thing.

Corina and her parents were there at one o'clock when we arrived. The Hawkins' were thinking in the same direction that I had mentioned to Milo earlier. All agreed that, the more trusted heads we had, the better decisions we would make on each issue discussed.

I was delighted and excited to see Corina, as well as Harper, but she too spent her time with Harper and Lil. I was allowed to watch, but even then only part of the time. I was used to being Harper's focal point and this was quite a change. Occasionally, the threesome would dash off to Harper's room for some mysterious reason. In several ways, I was glad and proud of the two, as Lil needed the attention as much as I did. This was probably an even more significant change for Lil. Regardless, I still wanted to know two things from Harper: would she really allow me to "comb over hair and kiss" her as mentioned on the phone, and when could I have some quiet time with her?

Before we arrived, Mrs. Hawkins had only guessed about whether we needed a meal or not, so she had prepared lunch. Once she found out that we had eaten, she put some of the main items away and brought out dessert plates. We ate cake and ice cream after the group conducted the first hour of business.

Mrs. Hawkins had pulled extra chairs into their large family room and set them around the two sofas that were already there. She acted as though she had hosted hundreds of meetings and events. She created an atmosphere that simply said this is how problems are handled. It also said, we will get through this, and we will still be okay when we are done. We will talk together, work together, and trust together. I was amazed at the sense of comfort and order even as the group talked about difficult and confusing matters. The peace and security in their lives seemed to set the tone for when life wasn't peaceful around them. I'd never known about this kind of decision-making process, especially when dealing with a problem. I knew all about dysfunctional, but little about functional, except maybe when it came to school.

Even the beginning of the meeting was, to me, unique. Max led off with a prayer. His prayer was simple and short, like Milo's breakfast prayer, but it had depth. It made me feel like I was in a holy place, even though I'd rarely been in one. I didn't get it. It was just a house and just a meeting, but it reflected a totally different perspective and made me feel that Lil and I were important.

Mrs. Hawkins sat next to me on one of the long sofas. During his prayer, Mr. Hawkins sat in a recliner, and I guessed that it was his preferred choice. After the prayer, however, Mrs. Hawkins caught his eye. He promptly changed seats and sat down on my other side.

As we started, Mrs. Hawkins asked me to call her Lucie. I was uncomfortable at first with sitting next to the two of them, but, in the end, their presence was comforting. Lucie had a sense of when discussions were getting into sensitive issues. When these areas were on the table, she would grab my hand or pat my leg or even lean into me to give me extra support. She had a way of showing love and concern without saying a word.

At one point, after Mrs. Hawkins grabbed my hand, Mr. Hawkins leaned over to me and whispered, "Don't worry Buck, I'm not going to be jealous, at least not today." He made sure that the whisper was loud enough for all to hear. Lucie leaned forward and gave him another look. It was interesting to see their conversation of eyes.

Mr. and Mrs. Schuler sat on the other sofa and Milo sat in a chair where he could face the group. Milo had a notebook and pen in hand. He opened the discussions with a suggestion that he share a list of what he thought were the main issues to be addressed. He had listed them in the order that they needed to be decided. He then asked for the others to add to the list. Once the list was developed, the group would simply go down the list and decide what to do, even if some actions were preliminary. His efficiency was impressive.

The adults often called him Mr. Logan or Michael, but he preferred to be called Milo. I think, for him, the name Milo represented a new identity, a re-birth, as much as a nickname. I think he knew he needed to deal with the baggage of his past, but it would take him time and, as importantly, it would take others time to see him as a changed man.

It seemed to me that some people go through a re-birth while others go through an early death. In some ways I felt like my mom died, at least to me, when she hit me over the head to protect JJ. Her body died later. I wondered if people could do both in a lifetime? I wished that Mom could have had the chance or taken the opportunity for change before it was too late.

As I thought about Milo's life changes, I realized that I only knew the new him. He told me stories of the old him, but even he struggled to reflect on those times and that other image. As I thought about Milo, his name, his past, and his future, I wondered about other people and changes in their lives. Then, on cue, I wondered about what changes, if any, were in store for me.

I was still feeling overwhelmed, but, as our time together went forward, I was feeling much less panicky. The group certainly shared and even took over some of my burdens. I felt a sense of relief after each decision was reached, and interestingly, I felt the relief both physically and emotionally. That feeling was especially noticeable after someone volunteered to complete a certain task or after someone said they would cover an expense and get paid back later, maybe.

Movement on each issue and down each pathway seemed to flow along as fast as the coffee was poured. Max would handle all the funeral arrangements. He would cover the costs for a simple casket, a short notice in the paper, setting up a visitation on Wednesday evening, ordering death certificates, and arranging for the cremation of the body. If funds were found at a later date, Max's business would receive reimbursement. He was to keep track of all expenses. He would also store the ashes in case anyone wanted to claim them at a later date. Of course, I couldn't imagine who would ever want a box of ashes.

I never knew there was so much to do when someone died. I don't know what I had thought except that a grave was to be dug and the person got buried in it. It wasn't that easy. Things didn't stop at the hole in the ground, like I thought. In this case, there wasn't even a hole in the ground, only holes in hearts.

It was also strange for me to hear them continually talk about the body. It was no longer my mom. It was "the body." Even though I hated what she had become, it was a difficult discussion to listen to. I agreed with all that was said; it just took some getting used to. I wondered if I would ever get used to dealing with death.

The group asked if Milo could hire Ed Casey, the attorney he worked for, to file various legal papers. Max knew Mr. Casey and had a great deal of respect for him. Neither Chip nor Del knew him but had heard good things. Milo indicated that the legal matters could end up covering a lot of territory and that some items in the future might need a different person, but Ed was the right place to start. One of the legal issues to be considered involved filing papers in Probate Court to consider an estate plan and to look at what Milo called the "child custody issues". Milo said something about the word "adverse", but I didn't know what he meant. That probate activity could look into my mom's work benefits, could look into any insurance claims from the wreck, and could appoint someone to do all the business of the estate, like pay bills, if money did show up. Milo called this person something, but I missed it.

The custody matter for Lil and me went more smoothly than I thought, but only after a rocky start. Neither Mr. and Mrs. Hawkins nor Mr. and Mrs. Schuler knew about JJ beating up my mom and me, or about Mom hitting me. Also, neither knew about the fact that I had been living with Milo and not "just visiting". When they heard this, Harper and Corina got called down and asked why they hadn't been told. I would have answered that, but I had gone to the restroom. When I got back, I saw a mini-inquisition being conducted. I jumped in and assured all that I had made them promise not to tell and explained what I was worried about. I also said that they could be proud that their daughters were so trustworthy.

At first, they only reluctantly agreed but, in the end, they also told the two girls that they were proud of them. Then, they shot me a frustrated look, and Mrs. Schuler said, "You know you should have told us. We could have helped." The other adults agreed, but Milo came to my defense. He clearly explained how my survival skills had kept me alive up to that point, and that I was just taking normal steps for the circumstances. In a new environment, this could change, but my survival mode was who I was, and they should be proud of me, too. That put an end to that debate and the group went back to deciding who was going to take care of Lil and me.

When the custody discussion got back on track, I was startled when Mr. and Mrs. Schuler jumped in and said that they thought that only Lil should come to the Hawkins home for three reasons. They said that with me dating Harper, it would put both Harper and me in an awkward position living in the same house. Also, with only Lil, Lil could have her own bedroom. Finally, although they realized that it would be best for Lil and me to be together, they thought the best option was for me to be very close by. With that explained, they went on to say that they really wanted me to be with them. Amazingly, they were already planning some renovations that would make that an easy adjustment. It was really cool to hear someone say they wanted me. I couldn't recall ever having heard that.

Chip provided details regarding the renovation. His original plan was to create an extra room to be used as a guest bedroom and as office space. The plan was to build it by expanding and converting the attic space that was over their attached double car garage. He and Del now wanted that new room to be my room. All that he needed was some elbow grease, as he called it, from others, but he needed no funds. Again, he had planned to do it anyway.

Chip went on to say that all he needed to do was to put in a door off the upstairs hallway, add some extra insulation, run electrical, and install flooring, walls, windows, and vents.

Max sarcastically said, "Gee, is that all?" The group laughed and, as the laughter ended, the group took a much-needed break.

Adding a room for me did sound like a lot of work, but Chip said he had done bigger projects and was anxious to start. He said he would love to have me around. I was ecstatic. Up to that point, my life had been measured by my abilities to escape and survive and I was proud of my skills. I wondered how I'd deal with another change in life that might expect me to adjust again and to possibly make additional changes. I couldn't really describe the new skills required, but I was confident that I could handle just about anything that life could throw at me. Surely, after all I'd been through, I thought changes like these should be easy. At that time, little did I know that adjustments to good circumstances could be just as difficult as adjustments to bad situations.

Either way, at that moment, I thought that I couldn't have picked a better place to live, unless it had been with Milo. I knew Milo would have been interested, but I also knew that it wasn't practical for me to be with him. Besides, he had his own living arrangements to work out.

When we got back together to finish the custody discussion, Corina and Harper rejoined the group. They had been given an update on Chip and Del's offer, and they wanted to put their comments and conditions on the record.

Corina said, "Buck, you will not be allowed in my room, ever. Do you get it?"

"Well, why would I even want to go into your room?"

"Just say, you get it!"

"Ok, I get it."

Harper pitched in and said, "I agree, Buck. Also, when she's on the phone with me, you are not to listen. Get it?"

"What is this with all these rules? What happened to the trust?"

"Being this close to us, changes the rules," said Harper. "And, that's just the way it's going to be, so just get it and get on with it."

By this time, the adults were all laughing, while I sat feeling like the odd man out.

I thought that I would define my rules, my role, and my behavior as I fit myself into these new arrangements, but, all of a sudden, I sensed that I didn't have as much control as I thought. These people were the same as they were moments before, but our relationship was somehow dramatically changing. I needed to quickly catch up on how to function within this new system. I wished there was a book to read that would tell me how to adjust, but I doubted that one existed.

In the midst of my confused look, Max put his arm around me and said, "Buck, I can guarantee only one thing, and that is that these two rules won't be the last." The group laughed again.

The only good that came of this was that Harper and Corina both came over to me and gave me a hug. During the hug, Corina said, "Welcome home, bro."

I said, "Oh, okay. I get it." Of course, I lied. As the coming weeks progressed, I would realize that Max was right and that there was a lot more that I had "to get."

At one point late in the meeting, Milo told our teen group and Lil to get lost for a while, so we left the room. The only words that I heard as we went into the den was, "looking into a wrongful death action". I understood some of what that meant but not all, and I really didn't care. I was so exhausted from the other discussions and so exhausted from thinking about my future, that I really didn't want to know more.

It was enough for me to think about Lil and me living with different people in different places. The whole picture was beginning to develop and from what I could see, it looked great, but it also looked so different.

135

Again, I didn't know how I would react to all of it, and I was nervous about what I didn't know. I wondered if I would still be able to be friends with all of these people. It was already clear that they would act differently towards me, but would I still be accepted for who I was, and could I even handle being in a family that actually acted, well, normal? Thinking about all the unknowns made me dizzy.

I wondered if sometimes the known bad is easier to deal with than the promised good, because one knows the extent of the bad, but still doesn't quite trust the unknown, whether it seems good or bad. I tried to remember a quotation about the "devil you know", but couldn't quite remember the exact words. Anyway, I wondered if it was appropriate for how I was feeling.

The meeting wrapped up and Milo gave each couple a list of notes that summarized the decisions and actions steps. Again, he was quite the professional. Milo was the only one who seemed to have energy remaining. In fact, he actually looked better at the end of the meeting than he had at the beginning. He seemed to gain strength over the day. He seemed confident and had a look of satisfaction on his face. He looked the same way I felt when I knew I had done well on a test at school. Anyway, I gave him a man-hug, which involved more backslapping than hugging, and I told him thanks.

Lil stayed with Max and Lucie that night, but before nightfall, they wanted to go back to the apartment with her to pick up some additional personal items and clothing for the week. Harper and her mom made it clear that one suitcase full of personal items wasn't going to do. When I asked, "Like what does she need besides what she brought?" They gave me a disgusted look, but I choose to ask no further.

I went back to Milo's tent that night but on the way, Milo and I met up with the Hawkins' family and Lil at the apartment. Some additional papers like health insurance cards were recovered, and Milo turned over the birth certificates that he had retrieved earlier. Max and Lucie were mostly tight-lipped about the condition of the apartment. The only time they mentioned anything was while going into my room to tell Harper they needed to go. She was sitting on my bed with a blank stare while holding one of my pillows. At that point, her parents mentioned how clean and tidy my room was.

As for me bunking at the Schuler's home, they needed another day to make some temporary adjustments, especially to the large bedroom of Corina's brother, Mark. I was to start staying with them that next night, even though the new room would take a few weeks to complete. In the meantime, I would have to sleep in Mark's room on a mattress on the floor for a little bit. As I remembered from the hospital, "a little bit" can mean many things.

Milo would get with Ed Casey the next day to see what kind of temporary custody papers could be issued pending possible future court hearings.

Lil and I decided to go to school the whole week. Lil needed to go to school for several reasons. Emotionally, it would be good for her to stay in a routine, and she needed to be in school because she was behind in several classes. Mrs. Hawkins planned to visit Lil's school as soon as she received the temporary custody order.

I didn't need any prompting to go back to school immediately. School was one of my favorite places to be. I loved learning, and I loved talking with teachers. I also felt that I owed Mrs. Sheppard an update. I anticipated the environment at school to be the same as before, but it wasn't.

Students, friends and just kids that I knew, reacted to me differently because of Mom's accident and death. I think many of them struggled with the death issue and their comments reflected their mixed bag of thoughts. It was interesting, but also uncomfortable. As the week went on, it got better, but it was an odd feeling. The only interesting part for me was noting the variety of reactions.

As students walked towards and past me, many just stared and whispered. They would make comments to each other like, "That's the kid whose mom was killed in that drunk driving accident." Their eyes never seemed to meet mine. Only once did I overhear a really sick comment. One kid said to another, "You realize both of them are toast. He's in jail and she's in hell. Ain't no forgiveness for them." I wondered how they could be that insensitive. No matter what they believed, Milo would have said that they hadn't yet reached the point of wisdom.

Other students, though, would stop and give me a hug and say how sorry they were. Even they seemed uncomfortable. These kids usually walked on quickly after the hug and departed with an awkward comment, like, "Well, I need to get on to class." If the shoe had been on the other foot, I would have probably been like that.

There were also some who would nonchalantly say, "Hey, Buck, you're in our thoughts and prayers." I didn't really sense any commitment behind many of those comments, even though they were nice to hear. Their comments reminded me of Manny's style and what I called the "bless and run" method.

There were very few, however, who really seemed to understand the confusion and grief that one might face when losing a mom. They hugged me, sat with me at lunch, wrote me notes and stuck them to my locker, handed me cards, and one even gave me a candy bar with a note. These kids stuck with me the whole week and asked what they could do. Maybe they didn't get everything about death, but they seemed to know a lot about life and the importance of caring relationships.

Wednesday evening was the visitation, as Max called it. I mentioned it to a few kids and called it an "open house" and once even called it an "open casket" event. When talking about it, I struggled with words and sounded like Harper after her stroke. I just didn't get the funeral lingo. Obviously, because of the condition of my mom's body from the wreck, it was not an open casket.

The fact that it was not an open casket made some of the people from The Cisco Tavern mad. Some of Mom and JJ's drinking buddies all tromped in together right at 5:30 when the visitation was scheduled to begin. They signed in and went up to the casket in mass. Although Peggy, Max's employee who I had met previously, had greeted the group at the door, Max saw them and greeted them again at the casket. They loudly complained that they needed to see her to say goodbye. They even pulled out a bottle and said they wanted to have one last drink together. Max refused to open the lid, and, finally, the group got the message. They had their drink around the casket anyway.

Before leaving, one of the group members mentioned how drunk JJ was the night of the accident and even mentioned that JJ and Mom had been arguing while still at Cisco's. Milo overheard this and heard someone call him Jack. Milo got the last name from the registry and made a note of it. I asked Milo why he was doing that. He chuckled and said, "I think

Jack just volunteered to be a witness in some future court cases. I'll also have some others make a note about what he said. I'll tell you later how it can be helpful."

Not once did I see the Cisco group look my way. I felt an intense anger towards them and said to Lil, "People like that are not friends. In fact, they're more like the enemy. We need to remember that Lil. If they had been real friends, they wouldn't have let Mom get in that car with JJ." As I watched the Cisco group, my anger and hatred for how Mom and JJ had treated me started to boil. I saw them as scum and had the urge to take the whole group on right then and there. Lil sensed my mood, saw my fists clinch, and felt me take a step in their direction. She grabbed my hand before I could take a second step, looked up and meekly said, "Please, Buck, not now. I don't want you to get hurt." Her words and expression stopped me in my tracks. I realized that I wasn't thinking about anyone, including myself. I hugged Lil and turned away from the group holding court by the casket. I couldn't stand to look at them.

Thanks to Lil, my anger was once again stuffed into some sort of emotional pocket for the time being and, eventually, the Cisco circus departed. After they left, a few of my school friends came in briefly and said "hello", but overall, the turnout was sparse. There were no neighbors, no Manny, no family besides Lil and me, no management from the Wright Company, and only one co-worker from her job. The people who did come, not counting the Cisco group and the students, included Officer Whales, the Hawkins' family and a few of their close friends, the entire Schuler family and a few of their close friends, Milo and a guy from the homeless camp called River Ralph, and a small group of staff from Summit High School. That last group included Mrs. Sheppard, Mr. Smith, and Mrs. Andrews. I spent more time with them than I did with anyone else.

I was only a bit surprised that Aunt Lupe hadn't come. Of course, as I remembered, she and Junior, her husband, seemed to only show up when they needed something. I hadn't seen them since Mom and JJ hooked up. If they had seen the obituary and thought there was money to be had, they would have come. I guessed they thought there would be unpaid expenses instead of extra funds. Still, I thought Aunt Lupe would come. Maybe she was out of town. I had to wonder when and if she and Junior would ever pop up. Whenever they did, it probably wouldn't be to help. I was torn. It would have been good to claim that I was part of a family, but some families come with so much baggage, they're best when they aren't around. I guessed that Lil was all the family I had left.

Even with the sparse turnout, it was an important event. Lil and I both cried at times and it was good to cry together. We took time to remember Mom before she met JJ, and it gave us a chance to remember some of the good. For me, it took a lot of energy to remember the good as my last mental image of her involved the encounter with her and JJ. A picture of her yelling at me and pointing towards the door kept creeping into my head. Lil helped a great deal. She brought up trips to the DQ for ice cream and playing Scrabble on the kitchen table. We both wondered where that mom had gone. We knew that we would really miss our mom, even if we didn't miss what she had become in the end. I didn't deal with the issue of forgiveness that some spoke of, but the remembering and crying did begin to dismiss some of the hate I harbored. Yet, even that bit of dismissal only applied to Mom. My bags still contained plenty of hate and anger to go around.

CHAPTER FIFTEEN
Sorting Baggage

Near the end of May, just weeks after the funeral, Milo's action steps were getting ticked off the list like balloons being popped at a carnival. Temporary custody papers were in the hands of Mr. and Mrs. Hawkins and Mr. and Mrs. Schuler. Although the custody papers on Lil listed her properly as Marie, others, besides me, started to routinely call her Lil.

Also, the probate papers dealing with property had been filed. Milo called it the estate. Of course, when I thought of "estate", Mom's property never came to mind.

Regarding that property, Milo's prediction was accurate. Mom did have items of worth, especially related to her job. He found retirement funds, life insurance, and I don't know what else. On the night she was killed, I guaranteed Milo that he would find nothing beyond what he saw in front of him. He could have laughed at me and rubbed it in, but he didn't.

There really weren't many items of value inside the apartment. After picking out personal items, finding $112 in cash, and picking up some additional papers that Milo said were important, there was nothing left that we could use. The few remaining items, like furniture and kitchen stuff, had been sold. My address was officially different. I felt very different as well.

The biggest items still on Milo's list were related to the car wreck. JJ was still in jail, but he had only had a preliminary hearing on the charge of vehicular homicide. Even with the criminal case still pending, a conference had been held with JJ's auto insurance company. Milo had hopes of eventually coming up with a good amount of money from the insurance company, and he thought that the money could be enough for college for Lil and me. Additionally, he and Ed Casey were also looking into a lawsuit against the Cisco Tavern, but that was in the early stages.

From the point of view of the adults, things were getting done. I should have been happy too. I wasn't, and I let people know it. I was a real grouch.

At least Lil seemed happy. To me, she looked like a new person. She dressed differently, she acted like she enjoyed her new school, and she even talked differently. Just the fact that she carried on conversations with Harper and Lucie was probably the biggest difference. When I saw Lil with Harper, it was clear that she loved being with her. But when I was around, Lil seemed distant. I couldn't figure it out.

One day, while Harper was over visiting Corina, I decided to ask her about Lil.

"Hey, Harpo, it looks like Lil is doing great. Are you glad to have her as your new sis?"

Wow, did I get a surprise response. Harper crossed her arms, got a disgusted look on her face, shook her head, grabbed Corina and marched out of the room without saying another word. I was left sitting at the table with Del. I looked at Del, stretched my arms out with my palms up, and said, "What was that all about?"

I expected Del to offer some kind of support for me. Instead, Del was rolling her eyes, staring at me, and shaking her head much like the two girls had done. In addition, she crossed her arms in the same manner. Then she stuck a finger out at me and said, "Buck you've still got a lot to learn. Would you like me to give you a bit of an education?"

I don't think I even said "yes", but Del acted like I had. She stood up and proceeded to uncork a barrage, and she seemed to storm in circles as she released the oration. I knew that loud and bold was how the Schuler family operated, but I hadn't been at the center of any of Del's full-fledged deliveries so I didn't realize what was coming.

"Buck Martinez, we've been waiting for you to ask about your sister. You know for as smart as you are, you are a bit of a dunce when it comes

SORTING BAGGAGE

to Lil. Do you realize this is the first time you've asked about her? Why haven't you sit down with her and talked with her and listened to her and asked her what she's been going through? You just don't get it do you? You are her big brother and you don't have a clue. Do you?"

Obviously, I didn't get it and didn't even know what "it" was. I was going to ask, but Del was just taking a breath. Corina had told me about how direct Del's lectures could be, but this was my first real encounter with the "buzz saw" that Corina had mentioned. I realized that I had best shut up until I could "get a clue" as to the source of her anger. I had never encountered anything quite like this. She was only getting started. I hoped I could catch up quickly, but the more I listened, the more I realized that I had stepped into something big time and that I was about to get a lesson on "it".

"When Lil got to Harper's house, she was a mess. She was the most depressed person Max and Lucie had ever seen. She had no friends and Harper finally figured out why. It was because she was too afraid and embarrassed to have friends. She knew she couldn't invite them over to your apartment, so she intentionally cut herself off from other kids. She was afraid that JJ would treat her like he treated you if she ever said anything at home, so she didn't say anything there either. She said she couldn't talk to you, because you would always run away to your room or the third floor. Eventually, she almost totally stopped responding to you. I think she was living in a protective shield of silence, pretending that she didn't need anything or anybody. She needed you, Buck, but you were too into surviving to see it. I'm not blaming you for back then, but you certainly need to see the bigger picture now.

"Lil needed her mom, but your mom was too into JJ and too into her drinking to see it. Lil needed help as much as you did, but she didn't even know how to ask or was too afraid to ask. When she got to Harper's home, she didn't even know how to be a girl."

I slumped in my chair while hanging my head over the table. My hands covered my face. I had never felt so stupid, ashamed, and sad in my life. More than any of these feelings, though, I felt guilty.

Del knew just what to do. She came to my chair, pulled another chair right up next to mine, and put a hand on my shoulder. Then, right after this rant, she said what at first sounded like the dumbest thing I've ever heard.

"Buck, I'm really not mad at you."

"Really? It sure sounds like it. You're right, though, I blew it. I had no clue what Lil has been dealing with. I was too busy with myself and with Harper and with being afraid of JJ to even think about her. I am absolutely an idiot and I can't tell you how ashamed I am. You all have every reason to yell at me and to be mad and disappointed."

"Well, I don't think I yelled at you, but I can see how you feel that way. No, we don't have a reason to be mad at you personally, but we do have a reason to want you to wake up to what's going on with Lil. She wasn't physically beaten like you were, but she was just as hurt by your mom and JJ. You need to understand that you were not alone in that chaos and not the only victim.

"I am angry, Buck, but I'm angry with your parents, and I wish that I could yell at them. Yes, both of them for not being there for either you or Lil. Yes, at times, I've incorrectly found myself looking at you as the responsible adult because you are so caring, but I know it's not your fault. Again, I'm not mad at you. This is simply the first chance I've had to vent to you about this. I had hoped you would come to recognize Lil's needs on your own, but I felt like I needed to jump in. Please forgive me if I jumped too hard. I shouldn't have been quite that direct. I'm just so mad at the world about this little girl, and you, hurting like this and having the hurt be so invisible. It just made me so sad and, sometimes when I get sad, I get mad. I have to admit that, at first, I didn't see her needs either. I was too busy with getting you settled and too busy with my family's needs. Again, I'm sorry if I was too direct. It just hit me all at once and you got dumped on. That's kind of the way we do it around here."

"Boy, I'll say. I've never seen you like this. Corina told me you could occasionally be this way, but I'd never seen it. Does this mean you have now accepted me as a full part of the family?"

I smiled and shook my head as though I was teasing, but we both knew there was a lot of truth to my statement.

"Mrs. Schuler, I feel way guilty. Man, I regret not getting this earlier. I don't know what to do." I paused. "What do you think I should do?"

I took pride in my survival skills, so admitting that I didn't know what to do was hard to swallow, but I really wanted to mend fences.

"Oh, Buck. You are one of the best. I like you all the more for saying that. You are just the sweetest thing."

"Do all women do this to men? You just kicked me to the floor and now you are saying nice things to me. What gives?"

"I'm serious, Buck. It seems to me that most guys would be totally defensive and not take any of the responsibility, but here you are asking what you can do. You are great and I think you are right to look at the next step. Here's how I see it."

She took a deep breath and started circling again. Immediately, before she could get started again, I warned her, "Del, I'm not sure I can take another episode of Del's dynamite."

"No, I won't do that again. I will be more careful with my words this time."

She paused again and then started speaking slowly and deliberately.

"As for you feeling guilty, I have my own theory about guilt and regret and what use they serve. In my life, I used to think of them as only negative, but I've developed another take on them. I think guilt and regret exist to remind us that, sometimes, we get only a few chances to do the right thing. It gives us a special perspective on life. It makes our opportunities with others more important and special. Each encounter can become an important personal intersection for someone. This importance adds meaning to each relationship in life. If we want our lives to be full and meaningful, we need to recognize these as opportunities and not just as problems. Regret and guilt serve the same purpose pain does. It reminds us to pay more attention next time."

She stood still and looked down. Finally she brought her speech to a close with one final, quick sentence. "Anyway, I'm not going to waste energy on feeling guilty. I know that I am forgiven and it's that forgiveness that gives me comfort and energy to move on to what God wants me to do, especially in relationships. I will let my mistakes teach me about the future, but I'm not going to get bogged down with guilt and regret. What do you think?"

I asked Del if she would ask Harper and Corina to come down, and if she would "let them in on my classroom experience of the past thirty minutes." She agreed and did so.

Even after this lesson and the encouragement of all, I still felt awkward, guilty, and like a grouch. I wanted to understand more about forgiveness. It seemed to play an important part of Del's life, but I just couldn't wrap my head around all of it. I certainly hadn't earned forgiveness. I figured I would only get what I deserved.

In addition to a feeling of guilt, I realized that I also felt angry, but it was different than the near rage I felt towards the Cisco group. Whether true or not, I felt like one more thing had landed on my shoulders, and I wanted to yell that it just wasn't fair. In the past, when I felt this way, I would run, escape, or retreat. I used any method to just get away, and others encouraged my efforts as requirements for survival. In this new place, it seemed the opposite was true. I was encouraged to be patient, work it out, share feelings, talk in over, and be responsible. It seemed like this new world was all verbal trouble shooting and in-your-face encounters with no escape possible. I was trying, and as hard as it was, I owned up to my part of the problem that day. Yet, overall, I felt like I had a backpack filled with an old world survival kit, but was facing a moving truck filled with new world problems. The old survival kit just wasn't cutting it.

After we all talked, Harper assured me that Lil was on her way to really being better and not just acting better, but she also made it clear that Lil had some distance to go before she was able to trust others and that she needed her big brother, just like Corina was needed by her younger brother.

Harper also told me that Max and Lucie had scheduled an appointment for some counseling for Lil and them, but the appointment was still a month away. Interestingly, they had scheduled the appointment with Dr. Guss because of the positive things I'd said about him. I wondered if maybe I shouldn't go along. I shared that thought with Del who said she'd mention it to Chip first and follow up with a call to Max and Lucie. I felt sure that Max, Lucie, and Harper would provide what Lil needed until the appointment, but also felt frustrated with the wait. Even though I had confidence in them, the new weight of guilt I felt wasn't relieved. Plus, I hated waiting.

As for me and as for the fact that I was still in the dumps, on several occasions I still just wanted to run away. I wasn't sure where I wanted to go or even why, I just felt out of sorts. I even missed being at Milo's camp. I had stopped thinking about "checking out" from life, but that didn't stop me from fantasizing about running away and becoming a Huck Finn. At least twice during this period, I went back to Sage Street, headed down the weed-lined path, walked through the homeless camp, and went to the edge of the river. I would just lean on an old stump, look out onto the peaceful scene, remember the past few months, and think about what life might bring from here on out. It was my place to search for answers and to escape, even if the escape was temporary. Of course, I had Big Red on my back and my Wolverine boots on my feet, just in case I decided to take off permanently. I never did, and instead, each time, I returned to the Schuler's house.

Several other times, I headed out the door in anger with no real plan, only to turn around and apologize. I would turn around more quickly if it was pouring down rain. In reality, my options for having places to run were disappearing. Milo and DeAnn's relationship was speeding forward at a faster pace than planned, and they had decided to get married within the month. When that happened, Milo would move out of Camp Milo and into Camp DeAnn. Milo was also working on getting his law license renewed. He had been given such good feedback on how he was handling matters with Mr. Casey that others encouraged a return to his legal practice as well.

I was glad for Milo, but I just couldn't seem to hold it together. I seemed to be frustrated by everything, even though none of it should have been a big deal. Every time I turned around, I felt like I was arguing over something with someone. Whether it was as simple as showing up for meals on time or disagreeing over the amount of time I spent on my new phone or as complicated as why I didn't want to go to church with the Schuler's, I seemed to be constantly in clash mode.

I was also already tired of sleeping on the floor in Corina's brother's room. My space was smaller than my room in the apartment had been. I didn't like sharing the bathroom with Corina and Mark, either. Corina even yelled at me for not putting the seat down. So, why was that my fault?

I felt like I had no privacy. Even when I did homework, I was out in the open at the dining room table with all kinds of people walking by and asking me things. I had no personal space and the remodel was taking longer than expected, or maybe longer than I wanted. I understood why it was taking so long, as I was helping to do it. I could see the amount of work it required, but I had run out of patience for all these little things that kept needling me.

As big as it was, the biggest challenge for me wasn't the space or the phone or the television or the meals or anything else. The one I cringed at the most was answering to Corina's mom and dad. When my mom was alive, I had been in charge of everything in my life and didn't answer to anyone. I resented Chip and Del asking me, "Where are you going? When will you be back? Who will you be with? Is your homework done?" I sometimes felt like I was on a quiz show.

One day, I got so mad that I yelled at Mrs. Schuler, "Look, you're not my real mom and you don't run my life. What are you, the FBI?" Her reaction was perfect for the situation and in dealing with me. Afterwards, I felt like a jerk. I expected Del to yell back at me, but she came to me, hugged me, and in a serious, gentle voice said, "This must be tough on you, but we are just trying to be responsible. We care about you and want to protect you. You know that's what people do with the ones' they love." Then she messed up my hair and said, "Now, you need to know that Chip and I will continue to ask you these questions. Oh, by the way, when are you going to comb over that hair?" Of course, she knew about this phrase between Harper and me, so she followed with a loud laugh. I loved her for her reaction, but I was still completely out of sorts. I wasn't sure that being loved was always fun or easy. Once again, I felt guilty, but I wasn't completely sure what I'd done. With my mom, I learned lessons by seeing the results of her self-destructive ways, but with the new women in my life, I was getting one verbal lesson after another. I hated my mom's lessons, but I certainly wasn't in love with learning the new way either.

Corina had witnessed the whole interaction between her mom and me. After it was over, she turned to her mom and me and said, "That's not fair, you would have grounded me for two days for yelling like that."

Del, turned to Corina and said, "You better believe it. Now, mind your own business," and she laughed again. Corina rolled her eyes.

I thought to myself, "What's with women and the eye roll anyway?" I still hadn't mastered translating all the nuances of those eyes. I returned to my private and not so private brooding.

SORTING BAGGAGE

To be honest, not all was bad. I loved the Schuler family, I loved the food, I loved the convenience, and I loved the way it had impacted both my work and school. School had always been great and it still was, but several little changes made it even better. I was closer to school, I could catch rides with Corina and my circle of friends had grown. I loved lots of it, but changing and fitting into their lives was way more difficult than I could have ever imagined. Again, I knew the anger I felt was different, but anger none-the-less and, sometimes, I worried so much about things that I felt sick at my stomach. My feelings weren't directed at others, like before, as much as they were directed at the situation. I hated how hard it was to change and even sometimes, I seemed to hate myself for having such a hard time with living in a normal home. I wondered why this was so awkward and frustrating. I thought there must be something wrong with me, and said to myself, "Maybe Dr. Guss was wrong. Maybe I am mental."

Things were changing on other fronts as well. I quit working at Manny's. It was no longer convenient. I still did some odd jobs at the funeral home, and I liked working with Max, but still, it was more change. In the past, I had wanted life to speed up, but in this new world, I often wished life would slow down and give me some time and mental space to get used to it.

Again, good was mixed in. Max also told me that if I could come up with a mower, I could mow his lawn at the house all summer. He mentioned that I could possibly pick up a few other lawns to mow in addition to his. It was a great suggestion, and I was trying to figure out a way to come up with money to buy a mower.

I liked the idea of having another summer job even though Mr. and Mrs. Schuler gave me an allowance that matched Corina's. I used some of the money I had earned at the funeral home and some of that allowance for my cell phone. I was saving the rest. Still, I hadn't yet figured out how to come up with sufficient cash for the mower, and I needed it right away. That dilemma represented just another frustration.

Interestingly, the week before finals, Mr. Schuler, bought a new mower. I asked him, "Chip, did Max tell you that I was trying to find a mower that I could afford?"

He smiled and asked me, "What makes you think you could afford my old mower? It's a high quality mower and doesn't really have that many miles on it."

"So, you're going to go used car salesman on me, aren't you?"

We went back and forth with each other and pretended to argue. It was such a treat to be able to tease and be teased by an adult. It made me feel special and grown up. I wondered if most adults understand that humor and allowing fun to be poked at them is one of the best gifts they ever give to kids.

He never admitted to it, but I told him that he must have known that I wanted to buy a mower, and finally, we got down to discussing the exact price. He actually charged me more than I thought, but I was just able to come up with the sixty-five dollars. Afterwards, he said, "Don't forget, you will still owe me for gas and oil." I didn't know for sure if he was teasing or not, so once again, I had to awkwardly ask for clarification. As he was walking away, he slapped me on the arm, smiled, and said, "Yes, but I'll let you keep track and we'll settle up in the future."

Even with the little things, communication wasn't simple in this new world of family.

In fact, being a part of a functional family seemed to involve a lot of work. I was constantly trying to figure out how to correctly fit in. I was trying to change and sometimes succeeding, but still, I often felt like I was the odd wheel and a step behind. I had never had to guess what JJ or my mom felt or what their words meant. Their words were certainly not subtle. With them, things had been consistent, bad but consistent. Again, this wasn't so with my new family. It seemed that I was constantly learning what seemed like numerous new and intricate dance routines. Unfortunately, I still had a habit of stepping on toes and was still learning the right moves. I was certainly a work in progress. I wondered if most families were like that.

It was interesting that the "work in progress" idea came up later that week. Due to a cancellation, and with some rearranging of his schedule, Dr. Guss called Mr. and Mrs. Hawkins and set up a time to see them and Lil on Friday. My willingness to attend was brought up. Dr. Guss was delighted with that idea, and he took it a step further by suggesting that all of both families attend if they were willing. He would set up the session in a large conference room. I was actually looking forward to seeing him again and was excited to have the whole group attend. It seemed to take away the feeling that Lil and I were the problem or the subject of the session. Harper even said that we should treat it like "our first family reunion since we were all sort of related now". She quickly realized what she had said and immediately followed with a smiling clarification. "Well, not related that way. You know we can still date and all."

Even though my first session with Dr. Guss had been on a Friday, that next Friday with both families felt totally different. It seemed more of a celebration than a trip to a shrink. Even entering the hospital was fun. As Chip, Del, Mark, Corina, and I entered we made enough noise to make people turn around. Someone could have thought we made a wrong turn and came to the hospital instead of going to a soccer match. Max, Lucie, Harper, and Lil came in right behind us, and when I noticed them, they were all laughing at the antics of the Schuler clan.

Dr. Guss had given us specific directions, so we quickly found our way through the lobby, up the escalator, and to the large conference room on the medical side of the hospital. Maggie, Dr. Guss' secretary, met us at the door and offered each of us a soda or bottle of water as we entered. When she saw me, she gave me a wink, a big smile, grabbed my hand, and told me how glad she was to see me again. She really seemed to like me, and I was glad. I asked her how she was doing, and she said, "I'm doing great, but feeling really fat and ready for this baby to get here," and she rubbed her belly as if to emphasize her point.

As I talked with Maggie, I turned to introduce her to Harper and Lil. Lil was holding onto Harper with a tight grip, and as I introduced them, Lil grabbed my hand while keeping ahold of Harper's. As we entered the room, Lil directed us to three chairs and said that she wanted to sit between us. It was clear that Lil was nervous, so I put my arm around her. Dr. Guss, who was already in the room, noticed this process, looked me in the eye, smiled, and gave me two thumbs up.

Dr. Guss got down to business by giving an overview of what he hoped to accomplish that day. His efficiency reminded me of Milo just weeks before. As he talked, his arms and hands whirled around in the air exactly like they had in our first meeting. He looked like an animated choir director. When he added his noisy cackle of a laugh, Max told him that he would fit right in with the Schuler family. Del laughed and told Max, "Oh, shut up."

After he spoke, Dr. Guss asked Mr. and Mrs. Hawkins to give him a complete update on all that had taken place since my mom's death. Max did most of the talking and he was awesome. He captured the events and decisions well, but what he did best was to share all the positive things that each of the group had done to make things work. He mentioned Milo's excellent contributions as well. Lucie shared her concerns about Lil and me and wanted to make sure that we were dealing with all this "trauma" in a healthy manner.

Dr. Guss asked about Harper's surgery and her rehabilitation. Max and Lucie looked at her, nodded, and allowed her to tell that part of the story. She seemed comfortable talking about it all, but showed the most emotion about the rehabilitation process, especially her frustration with her speech therapy.

Then, each person was given a few minutes to talk about their feelings, about how they were doing, and about what was the most difficult part of the changes. I could have predicted what most people would say, but I was surprised by two. Mark, Corina's brother, talked about how he felt left out and about how he sometimes was jealous of me for getting a lot of his mom and dad's attention. He said he liked me, but he was frustrated with all of the adjustments that were required of him. I never realized this. For the umpteenth time in the past few weeks, I felt like a jerk.

Then Lil shared. I was surprised with how sharp she was and with how she was able to dig down and really talk about her feelings. I nearly cried several times as she told her story and said things that I never knew. I don't think even Max and Lucie knew it all.

"I hated what Mom had turned into. I tried to love her, but she just ignored me. I hated JJ, especially when he tried to touch me. Mom didn't listen to me when I tried to tell her about JJ, she just cut me off. Finally, she caught him grabbing me all over one night and she put a stop to it. I thought when that happened, I would get her back, but she just went on ignoring me. She just spent more and more time with him and more and more time drinking. They walked around me like I wasn't even there. I used to cry myself to sleep, but then I just kinda crawled into my own shell and just vegetated. I wanted to do what Buck did, but didn't know how. I would cry when he would get beat up by JJ and didn't want to get hit like him, but I wished I could just run away with him. I never knew where to go and was too afraid of what else was out there. Buck had so many of his own problems…oh, Buck, I'm so glad we're safe, but I still have nightmares."

By the time she ended, Harper was crying and both of us had our arms around her.

I looked at Dr. Guss with tears in my eyes and said, "Lil said it best. Looking back, I think she had it worse than I did. Lil, I love you and I'm sorry that I wasn't there for you. I've spent so much energy being afraid and angry that I missed what you were going through and failed to show you any kind of support. Again, I'm sorry."

"Oh, it's okay Buck. I love you too, but I want you to visit me more often, not just Harper."

All of the adults had their turn to tell Lil that they loved her and promised to protect her. Even Mark was upset by what she had shared and acted embarrassed. I wondered if he felt like a jerk for sharing his jealousy. I knew all about feeling like a jerk. I planned to tell him later how glad I was that he spoke up, how much I appreciated living with him, and that I was the one in the wrong.

Dr. Guss let all of the discussions and sharing play out until it seemed that all had finished. He had listened and taken notes, but now cleared his throat and very briefly reflected upon what he had just heard and witnessed.

"I have several things to say. For one, you all are some of the most wonderful people I've ever come into contact with. You have taken love from the dictionary and brought it to life. Your caring fills this room. Your lives point out that love is more than a feeling. Loving relationships take work and effort.

"Secondly, I want to spend just a moment telling you about how similar Buck and Lil's situation is to some of my other clients who have just returned from the war. They are dealing with Post Traumatic Stress.

Mrs. Hawkins talked about her concern for the trauma each has been through and she's right on point. Buck and Lil have endured the most and will need support and time to heal, but all of you are dealing with the fall out. Buck and Lil, you have been living in a war zone and a disaster area and it seems like the sins of others have reached out and had a brutal impact on you. I too am sorry, but I see around you the makings of a great outcome. These people will be there for you, and we will all get through this. It will, however, continue to take significant effort and continue to require adjustments.

"That brings me to my third point. What we are now doing is much like Harper's rehabilitation. The word rehabilitation actually means to take action to restore something or someone to fullness or wholeness. Harper has shared that it's often a difficult and frustrating process, but it can lead to a great outcome. What we are doing here today is to heal the hurt and restore the spirit. Yes, we will have scars, but out of this very bad situation can come some good. The more we share and talk the better we will be able to talk about it and the more we will heal in this atmosphere of trust and love. In some ways, we are all restoration works in progress and work it is."

Wow! I thought to myself that he could say that again. He hit the nail on the head when he talked about how much work was involved in fitting in and how difficult change is. It was amazing how much he seemed to understand about how difficult adjustments would be. He actually pinpointed the very topics we had argued about. What was most interesting was how Chip and Del expressed some of the same frustrations. Chip said, "sometimes I'm just exhausted from the process of adjusting every day and wonder when things are going to settle down and feel normal." Gee, I could have said the same thing. Go figure.

The meeting or session or whatever it was called finally ended with some happy sharing and we all seemed to have appreciated the encounter and the opportunities to share. Harper and I talked after the meeting and joked about how we were called "restoration projects", but we knew that, in spite of our joking, it was true. It was good to laugh and good to look forward to our next family reunion with Dr. Guss, who was somehow becoming a part of the family as well. He certainly knew many of the family secrets. I wondered if he was a work in progress too.

CHAPTER SIXTEEN
Cutting Grass

School was out. I had lots of plans for the summer. Some plans involved school friends and, of course, I planned to make the trip to Harper's home and pool as often as Max and Lucie would allow it. That was only one of the reasons that made me eager to start mowing their lawn now that I had my new, used mower.

Max had a contractor mowing the funeral home lawn, but he had always mowed his own. I assumed that he was tired of doing it and thought that he could kill two birds with one stone: give me a job and relieve him of an inconvenient task. It sounded like a win/win. Plus, I would get to see Harper all the more.

Harper, like me, seemed out of sorts at times, but her reasons for being frustrated made me mad. Her issues, at least the recent ones, just didn't seem, to me, to be real issues at all. For example, one of the things she fretted about was, "How do I wear my swimsuit and cover this scar on my chest."

I suggested, "Let the scar show. Wear it as a badge of honor. Dr. Guss said we all have our scars." She didn't seem appreciative. Also, when Max overheard this, he looked at me as though he doubted my motive for keeping Harper in her two-piece swimsuit. I decided to stay out of that discussion from that point on. Once again, I discovered that I had a lot to learn about my new world surrounded by functional families. The session with Dr. Guss had been quite helpful, and I actually looked forward to the next one, but, once again, I realized that I still wasn't yet a pro at all the nuances of communication.

Still, I had learned enough to realize that I needed to drop my involvement in the swimsuit discussion and move on to the matter of the lawn. Max told me that it usually took him at least three hours to "do it right". I looked it over. I knew I could do it in much less time and was out to prove it on the first try. I didn't pick up on his "do it right" comment figuring there was only one job and one goal: cut the grass.

The first day after school was out, I pushed the mower the ten blocks to the Hawkins' house and planned all the way. By the time I arrived, I had the most efficient attack all mapped out in my head.

I was done in two hours and five minutes. I was beaming. I had wanted to break two hours, and almost made my goal. Next time, I would pick up the hoses first and not count that as mowing time. Mr. Hawkins was at work, but Mrs. Hawkins was sitting on the front steps as I rolled my speed machine around front. When I noticed her, I waved, "Hi, Lucie. I got it done in record time."

I was sure that she wanted to congratulate me and pay me, and when she invited me to sit with her on the porch, I assumed she was going to add a drink to the process.

"My, my, Buck. I think you may have broken some sort of record for cutting the grass. Why don't you sit down while I get us a drink?" By that point, I had learned that when a lady says, "why don't we sit"; it's really not a question. It's a directive.

It was interesting that she didn't mention payment. It was also interesting that she used the phrase "cutting grass" and not "mowing our lawn." Again, I was weird for noticing her words. Some people say, "Oh, it's just semantics", but I always say that, "semantics is everything." I realized that was an over-statement, but it made my point.

Lucie came back out with two glasses of water. "Let's sit down over here on the swing and talk for a moment."

It also didn't take a genius IQ to figure out that a "sit down" wasn't going to be a quick comment and a "You're outta here slap on the back." With that in mind, I tried to get the drink down and tune in to what she was going to deliver besides water. I wondered if she had some bad news.

Sitting down, looking serious, and talking seemed to be the signal of a problem in this new civilized world I found myself in.

There was the deep breath, pursed lips followed, and the delivery was made. "You know, Buck, the questions I always ask myself before I do a task are questions that relate to the intent of the task, the meaning, so to speak. For me, I need to know what the owner really wants before I can determine how to do the job. If I know and buy into that owner's purpose, then I'm more likely to share that owner's commitment and do it well. What do you think of that, Buck?"

"Are we talking about the lawn?"

"Why, you get right to the point don't you, Buck? Yes, I'm going to use the lawn as an illustration, but I'm not just talking about the lawn."

I was starting to feel like a kid and realized that, again, she wasn't really asking any questions. I sensed a philosophical discharge coming. It didn't look like the angry monologue that Del had discharged about Lil, but none-the-less, Lucie's style was probably just as potent. Honesty wasn't lacking in either family.

"Ok." My tentative word was technically a statement, but it was probably more of a question.

"Good. Now, when Max hired you, what did you think he wanted done?"

Slowly I inched out my careful answers. "You know, I thought it was just to get the grass cut so that it didn't end up over-grown and become an eyesore. I thought that he saw cutting the grass as a job that he didn't want to do, so he hired me. I thought that it would make you all happy if I did it as efficiently as possible. Somehow, I don't think you all see it that way. Now, I think I'm confused and need to ask, how do you see the job?"

"Well, I'm glad you asked." She took a long drink and set the glass down on the porch floor. She paused for a moment and studied the lawn. I thought she was telling me to look at it as well, so I did.

The next thing I knew, she was up out of the swing and touching my shoulder. "Buck, let's take a stroll around the house and take a look at the lawn and the neighborhood. What do you say?"

"Sure." Again, I issued a statement with a question mark on my face.

"Take a look over at that neighbor's lawn. What do you see?"

"It's beautiful. The grass even has a pattern to it. It's almost like they cut the grass twice and left a crisscross pattern."

"Good. I think you are exactly right. What else do you see in that lawn?"

I described the yard as best as possible and she complimented my description. She followed by pointing to a second lawn and went through the same process. Somehow, I felt that I was being set up.

"Thank you, Buck, for tolerating this conversation. I'm sure you are wondering what I'm getting at. Before we sit back down, I want to do one more thing. Let's walk around our lawn and take a close look and compare the neighbors' lawns to ours. Will you tell me what you observe as we walk."

I hated the walk. I was now looking at my work from a different point of view. It was difficult to admit it, but I had not done a good job. I noticed clippings that had not been bagged and realized the absence of any pretty patterns. Mrs. Hawkins pointed out missed patches along the sidewalk, a weed or two next to the flower garden edging, and clippings in the pool. She mentioned other, more subtle items too. For example, she explained how Max would always mow an extra strip past our boundary so as to be a good neighbor. The walk was humbling. In fact, that same feeling of guilt and regret that was generated from Del's recent speech started weighing me down again.

As we returned to the porch, my posture had slumped. I had gone from being proud of my speed to being embarrassed by the comparisons. It seemed that this new life and new world had a way of confronting me in ways that were more difficult to deal with than even the physical confrontations with JJ. It was uncomfortable and I was struggling with wanting to be mad at someone. Usually when I felt embarrassed, I ended up feeling like Del. I usually went from embarrassment, to mad, and on to trying to blame someone else. Lucie, however, read me perfectly and preempted my thinking. Del and Lucie seemed to have similar skills. I wondered if some kind of parent school existed and wondered if they were the top graduates. Also, they had similarly wonderful spirits. Still, Lucie continued to zero in on her point.

"Buck, many people, including adults, would have cut me off and not listened. They might not have been able to handle a feeling of being embarrassed or even mad about this talk, but I feel that you're the kind of young man that really wants to learn. I am so proud of the way you have listened. I'm also proud of the way you cut the grass. You really did break a record and it was your intent to please us and earn that money. The only problem is that you didn't know what we really wanted done. You didn't know our intent, our purpose. We have a reason for this lawn beyond keeping the grass cut."

She took another drink and rested the discussion for a few minutes. She had cut me off from feeling sorry for myself and from being mad, so I was now re-thinking about how to listen to her. I had to wonder if this wasn't an important discussion. I changed from cringing at her words to wanting to know her thoughts. I started to wonder if I was at one of those relationship intersections that Milo and Del had previously mentioned.

Much like some of the previous teaching lectures delivered by Milo, Mrs. Hawkins repeated and added to some of her points. I had told Milo that I hated his repeats and to just get to the point. Of course, he would then go into a separate explanation about how some ideas couldn't be explained in one quick sentence. He would say, "Some paintings need a bigger canvas than others." Like Milo, Mrs. Hawkins had taken out another paintbrush.

"Yes, Buck. Max and I don't just want the grass cut. If we just wanted the grass cut, we could hire a big farm tractor with a brush-hog on the back of it." She paused long enough to chuckle at her own words. "They could cut it fast and keep the length below the legal limits. There are a lot of people in this world that cut the grass just because it's the law."

She paused again before continuing in a gentle tone of voice. "You know, I think there are just too many grass cutters in this world." She allowed this comment to simmer for a bit before continuing.

"I share this with you, Buck, as an encouragement. So please don't take this the wrong way. Max and I want our yard to accent and to beautify our home, to reflect what we like, to enhance the neighborhood, and to reflect God's awesome creation. For us, it's just one of the places that might reflect our intent and God's intent, to reflect order and beauty in a world of chaos and ugliness. Buck, we look at how we live in the same way. Our meaning in life is defined by our owner.

"I thought you owned this house."

She laughed. "Well, yes, we legally own it, but I mean that we see God as our Creator and, therefore, Owner of all. Ultimately, at least for us, our identity comes from the One we serve, and we try to serve in a way, to do our tasks in a way that reflects the Owner's intent. Again, our overall meaning in life is defined by that belief and faith. We can only say we did something well, if we do it with God's intent in mind. What do you think of that, Buck?"

I hesitated, but, after an awkward pause, I finally realized that she really had asked a question this time. "Well, Mrs. Hawkins. I had never looked at life that way. I never made that connection. You make it sound so simple, but I had never understood anything like that when I read the Bible or when anyone else ever talked about God. I would always start with the Old Testament and get bogged down and confused. It would frustrate me so much that I ended up sticking that book into the closet. I've never taken it out. I don't know where it is anymore. I guess I need to have someone just give me the facts and tell me what the point is."

"I promise you, we can talk all you want, and Max and I can share how even we have struggled with parts of our faith walk for years. On the other hand, we really have discovered some important things. One of the most important discoveries is that the Bible is more than just an intellectual set of facts to know or technicalities to debate. Instead, we consider it a personal message pointing us to a living relationship with God. Now, I know that's a lot to swallow, but when you're ready, I'd love to share more. Of course, I need to warn you. Talking sometimes comes with risks and requires some trust. You will know when you're really ready to take the risk and talk about this in a personal way." She laughed when she said this and gave me a sideways glance.

I had no idea what she meant by being ready to talk. My mind was still on the lawn and with feeling embarrassed, so I kicked the conversation back. "Mrs. Hawkins, may I have another glass of water and after that, if you don't mind, would it be okay if I just did something simple and took another shot at the lawn?"

"Why, Buck, I think that would be delightful. What a wonderful thing to do. Max will be so proud of you. I'm sure he'll probably even give you a tip if you bag those clippings and crisscross that lawn like he likes it. You just seem to think of everything, Buck." She finished with a different roll of the eyes and raised eyebrows.

I chuckled and said, "Yea, right." She had been masterful. I needed to tell Milo to never face her in a courtroom.

As I finished the three hour re-do of the Hawkins' lawn, I shook my head and thought, "Well, Buck, I think you set a record, just not the one planned." I laughed.

When Max got home, he did give me a tip, even after I admitted how I had first approached the job and admitted that I had just been one of those grass cutters in the world. He really got a "hoot" out of my story, as he put it. He also added a life lesson, but it wasn't about the lawn. Instead, it was about the opposite sex. With a laugh, he said that the secrets of cutting grass had many applications in life. He readily admitted that he could never cover a topic or make a point with the same skill as either Lucie or Harper. He had come to a conclusion in life that women were often better than men when it came to communication skills. This led to a guy discussion about women speaking in eye language. It was another guy time that I had come to appreciate. I was only now beginning to realize how important these talks were. I'd never had them in my old life, prior to Milo, Max, and Chip.

In the coming two weeks, I wondered about the series of events with Mrs. Hawkins and her grass lessons. Regardless, I applied them to each lawn and with each homeowner I encountered. I arranged to mow three other lawns and was working on a fourth. With each owner, I asked what they expected and asked for details. I tried my best to deliver in each case. Most of the owners gave me glowing compliments and all but one added a small tip onto the agreed upon price. At first, I applied the lessons so that I wouldn't have to re-do any lawn, but the more I did it, the more I started to buy into the whole package and into the truth behind Lucie's lesson. It became more than just doing the right thing…it was like I started caring about the people as much as I cared about the job.

CHAPTER SEVENTEEN
Survive Or Live

The business end of my life was looking up. With my allowance, funeral home job, mowing money, and with Corina's parents paying for my essentials, I had no money problems. In spite of that, I still didn't feel like I fit in. I often felt like furniture that was out of place. Except during a few guy talks, I seldom laughed. My backpack was still a primary companion. Sometimes I felt like it was the only part of me that remained. I never told anyone else, but I occasionally even had private conversations with Big Red. I would say things to it that I wouldn't trust to anyone else outside of Harper. When I felt down, I would look towards it and say, "We can handle this. It will all come together. We're survivors."

I couldn't pinpoint any reason for my constant sense of feeling unsettled, especially since all the practical things in my life were going well. My room was finally finished, and I loved sleeping next to the open window on the backside of the house. I liked having a private place. When I lay on my new bed, I could listen to the sound of the breeze passing through the large Ponderosa pines that were just feet from my window. I felt secure in my new home and the food was wonderful. I still did my own laundry. It just felt right to do that. Again, I had no short term or long-term money problems. Mom's estate was taking shape and, between scholarships and the estate, I would more than likely have money for attending college. My relationship with Harper was incredible, but I knew she could tell that something was nagging me.

THE SECRETS OF CUTTING GRASS

I would be grouchy and she'd ask, "Gee, what's eating you?" I never had a good response. Sometimes she would say, "I'm here to listen anytime you want to talk," but I didn't know what to talk about. Even I wasn't certain what was eating me.

Milo wasn't around much, but we still had a special bond. He described us as being linked as outsiders and alien survivors who shared similar scars. I could call him and I was as delighted at hearing about the good things happening in his life as much as he was hearing about mine. No, missing time with Milo wasn't the issue either. When I told Milo how I was generally feeling, he suggested that I simply needed to dig a bit deeper and start asking the right questions. Once, he said, "Buck, I can't tell you something that you're not ready to hear, but when you're ready, give me a call."

"Milo, how can I ask the right questions when I don't even know the subject?"

He shot back with, "Oh, you'll find a day when it kicks you in the backside."

I just kept searching my mind and thinking. I thought surely I could come up with what was going on inside me and fix it myself. I could handle it. I'd survived up to that point and I would continue to survive. I was confident that I could do anything in life, if I just put my mind to it. My teachers had certainly told me that often enough. Dr. Guss was definitely helpful, but even his process didn't seem to erase this feeling of abandonment and sense that life had limited meaning. I realized that he was helpful in rehabbing or, as he put it, restoring immediate relationships. Still, I wondered about the restoration of the rest of me, whatever that was. Surely there was more to life.

I had also been thinking a lot about my mom's death. I missed Mom in an odd sort of way, but I didn't think I was dragging about that. In fact, I even felt a sense of relief from the misery of my time with her and JJ. The misery wasn't all over, though. Sometimes, like Lil, I had nightmares about life in my cell and being hit by Mom and JJ, but, still, things were much, much better. In fact, I kept going through my list and kept seeing all the things that were right. On the other hand, I felt that I was drifting farther out, and away from something important. To Milo's point, what was

I missing? What was I not asking? The increased complexity and activity all around me seemed to be fogging up my view. I couldn't seem to focus.

One Saturday, I finished mowing Helena Huffman's lawn and was sitting on her front steps. Although I was cooling off my body, my mind, as usual, remained in hot pursuit of answers.

Most people described Mrs. Huffman as a "Grouchy Old Lady", but she was nice to me and on that day, she offered me a glass of homemade lemonade. I enjoyed the drink and guzzled it down. I even felt comfortable with our "chat", as she called it. Her "chat" mainly involved her reminiscing about her husband, who had died two years earlier. Her face beamed as she talked about him. I couldn't understand why people referred to her as "grouchy". Maybe she simply needed someone to listen. I thought, "I'm grouchier than she is." I was frustrated. I wanted quick answers, but no one wanted to give them to me unless I somehow figured out how to ask the right question. To me, it seemed to be a classic "chicken or egg" quandary, and I felt it was another unfair development.

After Mrs. Huffman went back inside with the empty glass, I relaxed alone. I had no more lawns for the day and it felt good to let the air blow across my sweaty body.

As I relaxed, I again pondered my list of issues and tried once again to focus. I kept a list of potent matters that I deemed worthy of my wondering mind. The "secrets of cutting grass" and the implications beyond the lawns were kept near the top of the list along with the "what in the world is bugging me" issue. I also started to re-process the discussion with Mrs. Schuler regarding Lil and the subject of guilt and regret. I wondered if the issues were all connected and if so, how. As I wondered, I felt a strange sense of loneliness deep inside, and I felt that I was thinking with my heart that day instead of thinking with my head.

I thought about Max and Lucie and about a quotation they had once shared. "Some have wisdom beyond their years, while others have wisdom beyond the grave." I wished I had that kind of wisdom. Milo had talked about wisdom, too. He said a person only reaches the point of wisdom when they have the courage to put an important lesson into practice. These people around me were certainly wise, and I wanted to be wise like them. I just didn't know where to look or maybe how to look. I felt like I had spent most of my life studying experts in foolishness, but that history only taught me what not to do.

Family, friends, and a future career were awesome possibilities, but I wanted something even beyond them. The more I pondered, the more I looked at what the Hawkins family and Schuler family had, and whatever they had, I wanted. They were very different personalities, but they had several things in common. They honestly talked together, ate together, and went to church together. Each of those activities seemed extremely important. Yet, the most important link, and one that Milo shared as well, was clearly the unique way they approached the issue of the higher power. Each similarity seemed to evolve out of their commitment to their God, Jesus. If that was the main issue, I wanted to know more than facts about Him. I actually wanted to know Him.

So, maybe the key questions were, how could I get in touch with this mysterious Being, and if God exists and is so powerful, why didn't He get in touch with me? On the other hand, why would God even want to? What's He got to gain? Also, if He's so powerful, then how can He be so personal and let me ask Him questions like; why did you let these terrible things happen to me if you love me? Whoa! I guessed that these were maybe the right questions, but I wasn't sure I was willing to ask them out loud? Was I willing to risk opening up and risk admitting that I couldn't fix myself or fill my own emptiness? Were these the questions I needed to ask? Something in my heart answered with a powerful "yes", but my mind wasn't so sure.

I wanted to know more. I knew that the answer involved more than just "religion". Even my mom said she had religion. I knew others who claimed to have religion too, but I knew few people who were clearly living out their faith or belief or whatever it was called. I thought of Manny who seemed to treat God and religion like a superstitious person might treat a touchstone for good luck. My mom treated it and the crucifix over her sink like it was invisible. Others treated it like a philosophy to agree with at times and to discard if it became inconvenient. Comments kids occasionally made at school often made things even more confusing. None of these approaches would seem to add anything to my life, and each seemed like a waste of time and energy. If it was just saying I was religious, then the world could count me out.

I absolutely knew that these families, who had become closest to me, were different and not just religious. Their faith was like Milo's description of wisdom and courage. Their faith had become who they were. Their lives seemed full, meaningful, helpful, and happy. They didn't do everything right and they didn't do everything exactly the same, but they seemed to have a clear sense of what was right and important. Even more, they wanted to live for something in life beyond themselves and beyond their time on Earth. Like Mrs. Schuler said, with some things, we only get so many shots. I wondered if this internal turmoil represented my shot. Then, however, a sense of urgency came over me and, instead of following my heart, I, once again, tried to push it back into my mind and think it through.

"Come on, Buck. Just think. You can work this out. Just think!"

I worked my brain to the point where I felt dizzy. Finally, I said out loud, "Stop It!" I realized that at some point in life, I needed to stop wondering and have the courage to move forward and to at least take a simple first step. I needed to decide who I was living and working for, and I didn't want it to be just for me. I wanted to be more than a survivor; I wanted to thrive, to have a passion for life, and to understand who I am and, more importantly, why I am.

I heard myself say in a frustrated voice, "Okay, Buck, what should your first, simple step be?" If anyone had seen me wrestling with myself on those steps, they would have surely sent me back to the shrink. I asked myself again, what was my first step? Although I realized there wasn't really a step-by-step procedures manual that was a one-fit-all, the first step for me would probably be admitting some things. As soon as I started re-thinking about the night Mom died, I knew at least one of the things I needed to admit. As I reviewed that night, I was humbled. I found myself dripping tears, but not about her death. It was about something I had said and felt that evening.

Thinking of that night, I remembered giving Milo a guarantee that there was nothing except what he saw in front of him. Of course, he ended up finding a substantially valuable amount in a dusty shoebox hidden away in a closet. I thought to myself about how stupid it was of me to have come to that conclusion when I really didn't know and had not even properly investigated the matter. Valuable items were found, but only by

Milo, a helpful and skilled person who was willing to look and not make assumptions. He was willing to dig deeper. Harper had once said that I didn't know it all and she was right.

I needed help and I knew I needed to be open to asking about a matter that I had cast into my dusty shoebox and into my mental closet. The questions seemed to involve a matter of faith and a willingness to be open to something much bigger than me. It seemed like the hidden elements of my life's meaning were all connected to the answers to those questions. I had told Manny that I was not afraid to look under rocks and that it was the only way to find answers. Max had made a similar statement. Yet, for some reason, I was afraid to lift up my own rock.

Regardless of my fear, I was unwilling to make any more irrational guarantees that nothing else existed beyond the hole in the ground. I didn't have the answers, but I decided I had to ask. I had to be willing to take my first honest look at the faith stories of these people I admired. I also had to ask what could my story look like. My earlier positions about faith and meaning were taken without any search, without any help, and without any risk. I was ready to open up, risk, and trust. A voice inside me was asking for more. I wanted an understanding and a relationship that would allow me to make a decision to live and not just survive until it was my turn to fill a hole in the ground. I realized that I might never know every detail, especially about God or the Bible, but I knew enough to dig up the people who would be my sources of insight.

At that moment I was willing to look beyond what I could see. I thought about the first time I used a microscope at school. With help, I was able to see what had been there all along.

Suddenly, it seemed that my head and heart were united in the belief that a direction was within reach, and that this new direction in my life was related to believing in and understanding the relationship with God that these two families and Milo had. I would ask these people about their journey. I would admit I needed help with these first, most important steps. I wondered why, once again, first, simple steps seemed so difficult.

I felt like I was being shaken and jostled. I felt like I had just been kicked in the rear. Milo had said that this moment would come. On the other hand, I felt a sense of peace and a warm feeling, like I was in the midst of something bigger than me and in the process of discovering a wonderful treasure.

I knew just the right person to call: Milo. There were others I could have called and who I might call in the future, but I wanted to see Milo first. I felt I had the most in common with him and he had already seen me at my worst. I needed to ask for help and admit my past arrogance and share my new openness. I realized that I had come to the point that Harper and Milo had talked about. Others, too, had told me that they would be ready to share their personal stories when I was ready. I was ready, but I needed a starting point. Up to then, I had turned to my own intelligence and my trusty backpack to survive, but, again, I wanted more than survival. I was no longer willing to say that nothing exists beyond what I see in front of me. I was at that point where I honestly wanted to understand more than a subject. I wanted to explore a level of my life beyond body and mind. I was willing to trust someone to search my spirit and yes, my soul.

If I would open up and really listen while I allowed these people to share from their experiences and about how they approached the Bible, I might understand and see that "living truth" that they talked about. I might understand why they live like they do. Like Milo once said, take a simple step. In this case, the simple step was to decide and to accept that I didn't know everything and that I needed to look to find. I decided something that would change the way I approached life beyond any lawn. I decided to trust someone else to dust off my shoebox, look inside, give feedback, and hold my hand. I decided that some things in life could be true and right even if every detail wasn't clear. More importantly, I concluded that my life wouldn't change any truth, whether I denied it or not, but that truth could change me, if I let it.

It was time. I decided. With that choice and in that moment, my life suddenly tilted in a different direction. I was going to ask who owned me and who I worked for. Instead of focusing on "it", I was going to focus on "who".

I got up and headed home. As soon as I got there, I called Milo. From the tone of my voice, he could tell that I wanted to see him before the day ended. He came right over, and we went to a nearby hamburger place, found an isolated corner booth, and ordered two chocolate shakes.

Milo had a warm, welcoming smile on his face reflecting a look of understanding. He said only, "Sounds like you need to talk. By any chance did you get a boot in the butt?"

"I feel like I got more than kicked. I think I was tackled and stomped on."

"Well, just tell me what you're thinking and feeling. I know that you've probably reviewed and recapped every detail of the last few months. I'm sure you've got the questions ready, but why don't you start by telling me what you're feeling first and thinking second. Give me a bit of that review so that we can be on the same page."

As I stared at the table and fiddled with the straw in my shake, I started slowly to unwind my thoughts. Interestingly, as I poured out my thoughts, things made more sense than when I had rolled them around in my mind. Somehow, my rambled mix of emotion and thought took on a sort of logical progression. I retraced my steps and started to admit secrets, mistakes, and needs. It was scary, but, somehow, it also felt good.

"Before my mom died, I saw death as simply a means of escape from a dreadful existence. I saw nothingness as something that was at least not bad. I wished for something better, but if my wish didn't come true then I just wanted the bad to be stopped. I was seriously considering checking out."

"So, nothing to live for except to continue enduring the pain?"

"Right. Then, life around me changed. Suddenly, I found that I had everything I could have wished for. I had all the things that I assumed would make me happy. They were good, but I wasn't happy. In fact, I felt like I had a hole in my heart."

"So, Harper's had been fixed, but you had just discovered yours?"

"Exactly. Mom's death prompted me to wonder all the more about life for the living and life after death. I started to feel the need for more than survival and a need for more than just the absence of bad. I wondered things like, was Mom a special being and, if so, where had she gone, what had become of the person I had known. The funeral triggered all kinds of questions. It kicked off questions about me, as well as questions about her. Those questions became even more unsettling the more I seemed to change. As my circumstances changed after the funeral, my identity felt like it was being changed too. Whatever was happening, it involved more than a change of address. It also seemed like I couldn't get in sync with the changes. I felt awkward in this new world and kept stumbling. At times the changes were actually painful. I came to the conclusion that there is certainly life after tragedy, but I continued to wonder if there is life after death."

"So, where does this battle stand today?"

"Yeah, it's been a battle all right. Well, I think it stands this way. I don't think the missing piece or pieces can be found by me just thinking it through on my own. It can only be found if I let someone else look under my rock and it can only be discovered if I start by admitting some things. One, I need to admit that I do have a spirit side, that I've been arrogant and wrong about the faith issue, and that I need help in sorting this all out. I want to understand this part of me even if it means taking a risk of sharing, well, personal things. I feel like I don't want to wait. I think that I really do have a hole in my heart and that it's as much about life and death as Harper's illness. I want to live like Harper wants to live.

"For me, the biggest problem is how I'm scared to death of having to make more changes in my life. Change and adjustments have been so tough at the Schuler home that I don't know if I can handle any more. If I choose to allow God in my life, I just know He's going to want me to change. I can't imagine him liking me the way I am. On the other hand, I want my life to be more than just surviving. I want a promise that death means more than nothingness and an escape. I don't want my mind to go in circles anymore and just debate the meaning of life and death. I want to have that meaning."

Milo slowly rocked his body back and forth as he listened. Finally, as he smiled, he calmly and almost quietly shared. "Wow, Buck. You are way ahead of the curve on this. That assurance that you want, that promise, that peace, and that clarity are available. More than that, a relationship with Christ can actually take away many of these burdens that you are packing around. No man can carry all that weight. By the way, instead of worrying about the changes He might want from you, just focus, for now, on the love that He wants to give you.

"Let me tell you my story, the brief version. Let me tell you about my rocks I had to turn over, my bags that I had to unpack and my fears. Also,

I hope that at some point you'll ask Max to share his story. You might be surprised at some of the things he has to share that sound a lot like your story and mine. Especially the parts about our failures and fears."

Milo told his story. It seemed pretty long for the brief version, but it was wonderful and inspiring. It was powerful, clear, and believable. As I listened to the peace that he had, I was able to leave that evening with some of that peace, a peace that I had never felt before. I still had serious questions, but I knew I was on the right road. That evening, Milo seemed to listen, hear, and understand beyond my words. It felt like I had my own, personal, trusted counselor. He had been my rock throughout the turmoil of the past few months, and that evening, I began to understand where his strength came from. Milo ended by giving me a list of some logical facts and intelligent reasoning that backed up his belief in Christ. He explained that there were many more. I especially liked that part.

After my talk with Milo, I told him thanks and told him how important he had been over the past few months. He said that I was just as important to him, but he challenged me to look at all the others in my life who had stuck with me through thick and thin. He asked me to look at how those relationships had changed and grown, how each of those special people had been consistent in their commitment to me, and how their commitment to others like me was a part of their commitment to and relationship with God. Whether I had been mad, sad, needy, or helpful, they were there for me. I started to mentally list those key people and list examples. I quickly realized that the list was long.

The Schuler and Hawkins' families were at the top of the list. I thought about them late into the night even after I returned home. Yes, home. The whole process reinforced my desire to understand the foundation on which these people built their lives. How could they keep giving and caring regardless of the events and regardless of when the need developed? It was this courageous, unswerving willingness to be by my side that made me want what they had and made me want to give back in the same way. They professed to have that same kind of relationship with God and it was evident in the way they acted, in the way they prayed, and in the way they spoke. Their faith was not a pretend matter. I had soaked it in over these few weeks and I loved it. I wanted to be the same way.

The next day at breakfast, I mentioned my plan to walk over to the Hawkins' home and my intention to talk to Max. I planned to dig into what made him tick much like I had asked Milo to share about his inner workings. I was anxious to get going and, as I started out the door, I hesitated. I looked at Big Red and wondered why I was taking the backpack. I wondered if it wasn't just an extra weight that I didn't need. I took a step out the door without it, but I quickly stepped back in. It had become such a part of me that, even at that first step out of my safety zone, I felt naked. I knew in my head that I didn't need my survival kit, but emotionally I couldn't leave without it. I grabbed it and went on my way. In one way, I felt like a little kid grabbing his blanket, but in another way, I felt like it represented a connection throughout this life transition. My identity was changing, but I didn't want to lose all of who I was. Anyway, I wasn't ready to give it up. I wondered if I did fully accept or admit my faith in God, what would he want me to give up. As I thought more, I couldn't believe that a backpack would bother Him, but, then again, how would I know.

As I walked that first block, I remembered Del's breakfast prayer and how easily she had prayed about even the little things that were affecting her life. I had never prayed and didn't know how to start. I wasn't even sure I believed that God would hear me. Still, I felt the need to start talking to Him and not just Big Red. I checked to make sure no one was watching, bowed my head, and simply said, "God help me with my meeting with Lil and Max today and help me to start understanding you better. I want to know you like others know you, especially people like Harper and these two special families. I just don't know how to start. By the way, I want to keep Big Red close and hope you don't mind. Maybe I could take some of my things out over time and add some things that you want me to add."

I had called Max earlier and asked to meet with him and also asked if I could meet with Lil. I had asked him if he was willing to share his story, but I had also asked him if he would help me talk with Lil. As I was beginning to change my perspective of life in general, I was beginning to change how I saw others and how I defined relationships. I knew that my relationship with Lil needed to be stitched back together. As Harper and I had talked about it, she had used the words "heal" and "restore" and she was right. Both Lil and I had been damaged by the trauma of our home life and both of us needed healing as much as Harper had needed medical intervention.

A recent dream helped me see what my relationship with Lil had been like. Lil and I were on the same, shaky, swinging bridge, but she stood at the other end. I saw myself walking over to her side of the shared bridge. The dream detailed that we both had survived a storm on the unstable bridge that spanned a deep canyon. I tried to look over the edge, but could never quite see the bottom of the canyon. I also realized that she had been standing alone. We both had held on alone in our own way, but because I was older, I realized that I should have been helping her to hang on and to get across it. I had not helped, but at the end, I felt compelled to go to her.

The dream was impossible to ignore. I knew that I needed to start the process of reconnecting as well as continue the process of discovery. I knew that I needed to build new bridges with Lil as our days and as our relationship moved forward. I didn't need to worry about guilt and regret; I just needed to start another chapter in life. I needed to share, to listen, to love, to connect, and yes, to help us both heal, even beyond the sessions with Dr. Guss. Just knowing a few simple steps to take, like reaching out to Lil, allowed me to feel a bit of a relief from the weight hanging around my neck.

This whole process of searching and listening had given me a new focus and many new understandings. I didn't sense that my story would end with a "happily ever after", but I absolutely knew that my story would now include very different results from where it was once headed. I hoped that in the future, someone would be willing to ask about my story, and that I would be able to respond with the same kind of passion, clarity, and meaning that Milo had. I knew life was too complicated for "happily ever after", but that it was also too important to proceed with no hope.

As I walked towards Max, Lucie, and Lil's home, lose ends still dangled in my mind, but my purpose and destination for that moment felt exactly right. I didn't know about the next day, but I felt comfortable with the direction of my search. I was on my way to work on some of the most important yards in my life. They would be the yards of relationships. I wanted to hear Max's story and see how it matched Milo's.

I found myself walking more quickly and wondered why. Was it just the idea of hearing Max's story?

Oh, right, Harper lives in that home too. Thank you God!

My meeting with Max was awesome. He was so open and honest. As he told his story, he admitted that he hadn't always walked the "straight and narrow". He talked about his stumbles, falls, and failures. He even revealed that he had something in common with Milo: an addiction. It wasn't to alcohol, though. His was to money and to the world's definition of success.

"You know, Buck, once I would have done just about anything to make an extra dollar. I thought success was money and that being true to myself meant always putting myself first. Now, my relationship with Christ changes my perspective on life. I now realize that success isn't what I've acquired in intelligence, job, fame, or money. Also, I know that failure isn't measured by what I've lost from the world's point of view. The world's definition of success now seems hollow to me.

"The world tells us to be true to ourselves, but if that's how we're defined, what can we say about ourselves when we die? The missing piece in that statement is that we can only be true to self when we are being true to what God wants us to be. I have asked myself one question several times. That question is: What am I surviving for? The answer has led me to get over myself and on to others.

"Buck, I know that you're a product of God and that God has a purpose for you. So, being true to yourself means being true to what God wants you to be and true to His intentions for your life. In other words, the fullness of who you are involves more than you.

"Dr. Guss talked about rehabilitation being a process of restoration. He talked about body and mind and a bit about spirit. He encouraged us to talk about our feelings and to talk to each other and he was right. There is another person we can talk to as well, and that's Christ. Getting in touch with Christ is the first simple step to the restoration of your soul, your very essence of being. As you talk to Him, look to Him, and study the Bible about Him, He will become a part of your everyday adventures. When He does, you can be assured that your life can have eternal meaning and not just the temporary glitz or chaos or frenzied activities that the world might call normal. When the God of love comes into play, you will realize that you can begin to measure your life by what you give and not what you get. You already know that Harper goes to a Bible study and that small group is looking into the Book of I John currently. I think you should consider joining. For me, that's the best way to read the Bible and the best way for you to find your purpose in life. What do you think?"

His sharing connected the dots for me and tied together the verbal and living messages of Milo and two very special families. For each, the first step was their belief in the God of love. The God who wants us to live lives of loving relationships instead of a living hell filled with insane chaos. I realized that these people focused on serving and honoring Christ instead of just paying Him lip service. It was that first step of faith that unlocked the natural next steps. I wanted out of the chaos and into a new reality. Chaos would still be around, but I didn't have to live a life that added to it or allow it to own me. This new belief gave me a sense of feeling free. I was there.

Harper and Lil entered the room as Max finished and they overheard his last sentence about "purpose". Harper looked at me with a huge, happy smile on her face, came over to my chair, jostled my hair, kissed me on the forehead, and said, "Well, I know one thing for sure. Part of God's purpose for you is to make Lil and me happy, and if you're smart, you'll do just that. Get it? Lil looked just as happy and gave us two thumbs up." I wondered. Did I just have a prayer answered?

Discussion Options

As indicated in the earlier "Disclaimer", it is not the author's intent to accurately depict or recommend any mental health, medical, legal, social work, or any other professional practices. It is, however, the intent of the author to create a fictional work that provides opportunity and stimulus for thought and discussion relative to various formal and informal support systems and relative to the search by individuals for meaning and purpose in life and especially the role that our faith or lack of faith fits into this search. The following represent a few considerations that might act as prompts for such discussion. For young adult readers, some of these prompts might fit best in a group setting with an adult leader.

1. Discuss or describe how Harper and Buck may have shared similar illnesses/issues? Also, consider how they may have had similar reactions to their circumstances such as feelings of helplessness, impatience, or unfairness. How did each of them become a restoration or rehabilitation project? Describe how you identify with the two of them?

2. At least one character in the book suggested that good might come from bad. What do you think about this statement? Could periods or moments of crisis, pain, trauma, or turmoil have an outcome that could reflect an extra awareness of strength, insight, affirmation of belief, open door, or a transformation of faith? Discuss your experience or the experience of someone you know relative to this idea.

3. Consider discussing/describing your struggles with any faith issue such as prayer, death, hate, forgiveness, soul/identity, trust/expectations, purpose, or other. How did these struggles play out in the book with Buck and others? In what ways did you relate to any of these struggles?

4. Consider discussing issues and feelings such as guilt, anger, loneliness, hurt, identity, and attachments related to the story. Select one of these and discuss how it has been a part of your life. Have any of these feelings or struggles in life had an impact in changing you into a better person. How so? Do any of these issues relate to your faith struggles in question # 3.

5. Are wisdom, insight, and confirmation of truth in life sometimes available from unlikely sources or events? Do people sometimes follow patterns of repeated mistakes, which seems antithetical to wisdom? How was wisdom defined in the novel and how would you define it? Have you ever gained wisdom from an unlikely source? Have you ever been stuck in a pattern of repeated mistakes? How is this discussion similar to sin being defined as "missing the mark"? Does God sometimes utilize an unlikely person or source?

6. Consider discussing the idea of becoming a new person and how the concept of re-birth occurs in the book. Is it a process or a single event? Does it really occur? Has it happened to you? How were Buck and others different as the book and story progressed/after key events? Are there any similarities with these changes and with the Biblical concept of re-birth?

7. Do you think Buck really decided on anything at the end of the story? If so, what did he decide and why? What do you think about Buck's connection to his backpack? What kinds of backpacks do we carry and what might be in our backpacks? Was it okay for him to hang onto it even after he "decided" or does this indicate that he didn't change at all? How do you respond when someone says something to you like "all things in God's time"?

8. What does it mean to ask someone to tell his or her faith story? What would you share if someone asked you? Why did Buck specifically seek out Milo and Max to hear their stories? Is it true that some people verbally express the same exact belief that others express, but when it comes to their actions, they don't look anything alike. Does this observation make you wonder what constitutes a belief and if belief must go

beyond a generalized thought? Did any of the comparative characters exemplify this observation? Can we believe and not demonstrate loving relationships in our daily lives?

9 In the mental health field, one element to be determined during an evaluation could be: is a patient oriented in place and time? What does this mean to you and how do you think God wants us oriented? Does He intend order and not chaos? Is His intended order related to our relationships and our obedience? How do we have any sense of order if it's true that "normal", for the most part, is non-existent? If we are allowed elements of uniqueness within the norm, do these unique characteristics license misbehavior, poor choices, and lives of filth? Might spiritual health, relational health, and mental health have any connection, one to the other?

10 For someone in college who might be interested in going into social work, psychology, or medicine, it might be interesting to consider if the story related any indicators or patterns in child abuse and neglect, addiction, domestic abuse, MH issues, and/or family dysfunction.

Final Comment: This author is thankful for the elderly lady, who in 1961 in Savannah, Missouri, taught him a portion of the "Secrets" lesson. Over time, he expanded the lesson and has come to accept that there is but one Owner of his life, and that he can only measure tasks by looking to Him for His expectations. "I ain't always done it, but I've knowed it to be important."

CPSIA information can be obtained at www.ICGtesting.com
Printed in the USA
LVOW07s1051091016
507816LV00002B/7/P

9 780692 577172